DEAD IN THE WATER

THE WATER TRILOGY | BOOK TWO

BRITNEY KING

WWW.BRITNEYKING.COM

ALSO BY BRITNEY KING

DEAD IN THE WATER

BRITNEY KING

COPYRIGHT

DEAD IN THE WATER is a work of fiction. Names, characters, places, images, and incidents are products of the author's imagination or are used fictitiously and are not to be construed as real. Any resemblance to actual events, locales, organizations, persons, living or dead, is entirely coincidental and not intended by the author. The scanning, uploading, and distribution of this book without permission is a theft of the author's intellectual property. No part of this publication may be used, shared or reproduced in any manner whatsoever without written permission except in the case of brief quotations embodied in critical articles and reviews. If you would like permission to use material from the book (other than for review purposes), please contact

https://britneyking.com/contact/

Thank you for your support of the author's rights

Hot Banana Press

Cover Design by Britney King LLC

Cover Image by Christopher Campbell |chrisjoelcampbell.com

Copy Editing by Librum Artis Editorial Services

First Edition: 2017

ISBN: 978-0-9966497-8-0 (Paperback)

ISBN: 978-0-9966497-3-5 (All E-Books)

britneyking.com

For you.
They're always for you.

PREFACE

There's a girl not long dead who rests
down by the water's edge.
Her final words were, " Please. I won't tell—I —."
She never did get the second half
of her sentiment out.
I made sure she never will.
Some things are best left unsaid, I think.
In the end, it didn't matter anyhow.
I knew she wouldn't tell.
And she knew it too.

∼

There's a girl who rests
down by the water's edge.
She was young, but you
and the water washed it all away.
Sometimes I don't get why you
do the things you do.
But you like it that way— and in a sense, I do too.

∼

CHAPTER ONE

JUDE

AFTER

DO I LOVE MY WIFE? Of all the questions there are to ask —*this* is what the woman sitting across from me wants to know. It's a simple question, really. Which should make the answer simple. But then, the truth is far from simple, and in our case, particularly lately, the answer's not even close to black and white.

It wasn't always this way. But you know that.

I don't answer—at least, not right away. It isn't her eyes I watch as she frames the next question, it's her lips. They linger, moving slowly as she speaks, and it doesn't help matters any that they're painted a striking shade of red. This color is a stretch for a so-called professional, and then, of course, there's the other issue—the fact that her top is unbuttoned two buttons below what I'd consider appropriate. Still, I pretend not to notice. But that's not to say it doesn't take effort. Pretending isn't all it's cracked up to be. You know that too.

This woman, whom I'm not answering, she sits legs crossed, head cocked, and she studies me. I study her too. Because what else can you do when you're avoiding things? We're in a stand-off the two of us, and I'm familiar with this territory. It led me here. It helps that I find her interesting, from the smart blonde bob that frames her face, to her long, thin legs. I try to avert my eyes, and I do my best not to stare, although that is exactly what I'm supposed to do. It's my job to make eye contact—it's what she wants, it's the other reason I'm here. And in any case, I'm married, not blind, and I won't lie, she's attractive for a woman trying to get in my head.

This kind of woman is the worst kind. We've just met and already she's trying to dissect me, as though I'm some sort of specimen, and she seems to sense that I see her for what she is. I've known more than a few like her in my time. I can see what she's thinking as she sizes me up, peering up at me as though I'm some sort of alien. It doesn't matter that I'm silent. No matter what I say to her, it'll be as though I'm speaking a foreign language, and according to her expression, she's already decided that it's one no one has understood, ever. Whatever the case, I can also see that she's equal parts put off and intrigued. I'm wondering if now would be the time to tell her I already have one just like her at home, and I sure as hell didn't come here looking for another. But, then, probably not. Every man knows that some things are better left unsaid.

"Do you love your wife?" she repeats again, and it's amusing. I know I could lie. It would be so easy just to tell her yes, I do; it would be nice to keep it short and sweet. But I can't make myself say the word. Three letters could save me. And yet, I can't make myself spit them out.

8

You could. But you can do a lot of things. You can reduce a man to nothing. You've always had that effect on me. It's what landed me here, in this office, in this position.

Still, it's far from over. You can knock me down, Kate. But don't be surprised when I get back up. I'm not a quitter. You should know that. Maybe you've forgotten. But you'll see.

She sighs, and she's contemplating her next move. I can see the wheels turning behind her eyes. I look away. She isn't good at hiding her feelings, and maybe she's not like you. I shift in my seat, and suddenly my throat is dry, and I realize I'm still staring at her mouth. Also, I'm in trouble. It's just, well, I've forgotten how much you can miss a person's mouth. I'd forgotten how much I could miss yours. It's coming back to me, now, here, at the most inopportune time, and suddenly I'm trying to recall the last time we kissed. I can't remember. These days, we do other things. But not that.

She clears her throat, and I glance up and meet her gaze. I wonder if she knows what I'm thinking. I think she does. My dick gets hard at the thought of kissing you, at the thought of the way it used to be. She smiles because she thinks it's about her.

Women like her always do.

How hard a question is it, Mr. —" she starts. She pauses and looks down at her tablet. "Mr. Riley?" she finishes, and she meets my eye again. She's toying with me. She hasn't forgotten my name. This woman is smarter than that. I'd be stupid to think otherwise. Luckily, I'm experienced, not stupid, and this is a game I know well. Cheryl Edwards-Steinbeck, I study the letters on her nameplate and instantly my dick goes soft. Of course, she's one of those women. You know, the kind who can't settle on just one name. Such a thing would be incomprehensible for a woman like Mrs. Edwards-Steinbeck. Please, she'd say if her guard were down, one name is for plain folk, peasants—not a woman such as herself, one with stature. She has a reputation to uphold. She wants people to know she's married— respectable— while at the same time neatly stating that she's not dependent on a man, and she's keeping her last name to prove it. It's too bad for her that I know her husband, and he says otherwise.

She folds her lips and shifts just slightly. She's displeased with silence. But then, so are you. Maybe all women *are* the same.

I want to tell her how displeased I am that I'm here, now that I've come. I want to let her know how cliché it is that she wants me to think— hell, that she wants everyone to think— she's unique, an island all her own, when she isn't. But it gets worse. Now she's trying to portray a level of incompetence in order to get me to let my guard down. Women: give them time, and they'll show their true colors. One way or another, every single time. Despite my silence, I want to tell her this, too. But I won't. Because this particular woman, I'm required to see, and she and I, we're working on a points system. Which means in order to get what I want, I can't tell her what I really think. It means I have to tread carefully, and believe me, it's a minefield.

But it's not as though I have much choice in the matter. Now that I'm in this position, now that I'm going to need to be around more, it seems I have no choice but to give her what she wants. She's my ticket in. I sort of need this job with the firm. Even though I really don't. Although nothing is as it seems, though, is it? Like Edwards-Steinbeck here, people can call themselves whatever they want and it won't change the fact that a spade is still a spade. This particular spade, I might add, has done a very good job of luring me in. Which is in part why I'm avoiding and evading. That's a skill, too. But then you know a thing or two about that. I just hope

10

she recognizes this as a skill. I hope she sees how I am at holding out— almost as good as you.

But not quite.

This probing that she's doing, it isn't unusual; I don't blame her. It's her job. But that doesn't mean I have to like it. Unfortunately, it's par for the course in this line of work, psych-evaluations. Which is why, for now, I play their game. They want to know I've got it together. They need to know I can maintain control at all costs. Lucky for them, I am the epitome of control. But given that, right out of the gate, we're talking about you, not me, I realize that revealing much of anything in the way of the truth won't exactly play out in my favor. Not here. Not with her.

But this lady—she is relentless. So relentless, in fact, that part of me wants to warn her about the last shrink I spent time with.

Of course, I *could* just give her what she wants. As you well know— that much would be easy. In a sense, it wouldn't be hard to tell the truth, that yes, of course, I love you. I've watched you carry and give birth to our child. I've watched you love the one you didn't carry, more than life itself. But there's also a lot I don't know how to tell this woman. Things I can't tell anyone, especially not you.

THE THERAPIST'S PHONE RINGS, INTERRUPTING MY THOUGHTS. She doesn't stand to leave or ask me to excuse her; she simply holds up her index finger and takes the call. She isn't polite, and this irritates me more than I want to let on. As she chatters away, she glances my way every once in awhile, just to ensure she has my attention. She wants to know I'm listening; she likes to wield her power, this one. But clearly she knows nothing about manners, HIPPA, or privacy in general, and so she rattles on. I wonder how much her husband tells her. Are they testing me? Trying to see if I'll reveal too much? Surely, she knows what I am. Does she care?

As I study her features, I consider how much to give when she stops being rude and starts in once more with the questions. Maybe I'll tell her everything. Maybe it doesn't matter anyway.

For now, attention is what she wants, and attention is what she gets. Her nose is narrow; her chin wide, her makeup painted on and I decide that she is at least a decade older than she's trying to let on. For one, her pencil skirt is a tad too tight, and more than a tad too short. She wears it proudly though, and to that I say what the hell. If you've got it, you might as well flaunt it. Except she's in a position where she needs to be in control, and dressing like a high-dollar hooker makes her seem less so. But then, that's her problem. My gain. When she's satisfied that she has my full attention, she ends the call.

"Tell me about your relationships, Jude," she says, and I haven't given her permission to use my first name. We aren't friends here— this is business— but then women like her aren't the kind to ask for permission. I eyeball the rock on her finger, and I offer my slyest smile. She waits patiently for an answer.

"Tell me about yours, Cheryl," I say, and her eyes follow mine to her left hand. She's mildly amused. But she hides it well. It could be the three coats of makeup, though; it's hard to tell.

She laughs, and I know my assessment was right. She's bored—with life, with work, in general and she wants to play. "That's a story for another day, Mr. Riley," she chides and suddenly she's back to formalities. Despite her inherent sense of desperation—she can read people; I'll give her that.

She glances down at her tablet again. "I see here that your wife filed for divorce several years back," she says and this one, she's ruthless. Although, I have to admit, I do appreciate the way she chooses her words carefully. These things can be life-saving.

"Really," I tell her. It isn't a question, but more of a statement. It's a word that means nothing, and yet it saves lives in this moment. It buys us both time.

"Really," she answers and then she deadpans. I watch as she glances back at her tablet, and I can tell that I make her nervous and unsure, even if she's not willing to show it. "Although... it was never completed," she adds, looking up at me. She raises her brow. "The case was withdrawn from the courts... can you tell me about that?"

"I'd rather not."

"And why is that?"

I try honesty on for size. "It's painful."

She frowns and it's obvious she doesn't buy my answer, which is really too bad. Finally, she exhales. "Ah, but Jude—you see, that's what we're here for. It's important to get to the bottom of things."

"Couldn't we give waterboarding a try instead?"

She laughs, but only a little. Then she lowers her gaze and then her voice. "In that case," she says. "I think it's time you bring her in."

I don't laugh. I don't say anything. I don't know what I was expecting her to say.

But it certainly wasn't that.

~

CHAPTER TWO

JUDE

BEFORE

"What's the secret?" Stanley asks, and you look over at me. "You guys look so happy," one of the women follows. "Yeah—" her husband chimes in. "It's like you haven't lost it—if you know what I mean," Stanley interrupts drunkenly. I watch as he drunkenly takes another swig of his fourth whisky. He places his glass on the table and eyeballs you. "So, don't hold back," he urges and he slurs heavily as he speaks, clearly not one to quit while he's ahead. "Tell us the secret."

You smile politely, because it's not a new question for us; it's what people always want to know. You're thinking what I'm thinking: these people, they want a quick fix. They're the epitome of everything that is wrong with society. They think there's some magic pill you swallow that will make marriage anything but that which it is—work.

"There isn't one," you admit shyly, and I love watching

you in this light. It pleases me the way you lift your napkin and fold it carefully before replacing it neatly in your lap. You're all in tonight; I can tell by the way you pause demurely when you speak, even though you're anything but. You're putting on a show, and it just so happens to be the kind I like. I look over at you, and you can't know how happy you make me. You're poised and in control, and you answer so I don't have to. I appreciate that. "I just chose really well," you eventually relent, and it's a confession, but you're beaming, and you know how I hate having all eyes on me. I also happen to hate weddings and most people, but even so, it's this version of you I enjoy most. You're in rare form tonight; you're playing 'agreeable Kate,' the one who only shows herself whenever she has an audience, whenever our so-called friends are around. They aren't our friends, they're our neighbors, and proximity isn't the same thing as close. I don't want to break your little heart, and tell you that these people couldn't give two shits about you, about us, or about anyone really, other than themselves. Instead, I let you believe and maybe *that's* the secret.

"You guys *are* perfect," our neighbor Josie says to us, but mostly to the other eight people seated at our table. "A match made in heaven," she adds, and you excel at having her do your bidding for you. I watch as you fiddle with the strap on your dress, nudging it back onto your shoulder, and then your eyes meet mine. You know as well as I do the importance of influence, of social proof, you're aware how keen these boring hags are to have the same opinion about anything and everything. Except when they don't. "Well, no one's perfect," Anne offers.

"Yeah, but look at them," her husband Stanley pipes up. "They can't keep their hands off each other—they even ordered the same thing off the menu, so I'd say they're head over heels for each other..." He looks around, making sure it's understood that he's openly disagreeing with his wife. After all, it was Stanley who started this whole thing. And just when I'm beginning to think there's no worse tactic to get yourself laid, he goes on. "And you know how I feel about gushy stuff."

"We work at it," you assure them, waving them off, eager for their attention to fall elsewhere. But not really. You know as well as I do that it doesn't hurt that these people think we're perfect. It means they keep their distance, at least to an extent. For that reason, we let them believe—it makes it easier to hide in plain sight. That's the thing about people: they want to believe. People want hope. But not me. I want truth.

Truth is difficult though, in our case. Even I know that. Most people either aren't ready for the truth, or they can't handle it. Truth can get you in trouble— my father is famous for those words. He just never much liked it when I or my mother threw them back in his face. But he was right. If the people seated beside us knew who we really are, beneath that little black dress and this goddamned bow tie, they'd head for the hills, and it doesn't escape me that it might actually be the best thing. Of course, they can't know. And so, we continue to craft our façade, and it's all politics, this business of trying to be a normal couple, a normal family. We tread carefully, we always have. We say the right thing, we do the right thing, and after a while people stop asking questions. They move on—after all, we look bloody perfect, and you know what perfect does? It hurts those that aren't. Take your friend Anne, for example. That's why she's sitting with her arms crossed, bottom lip out. She's pissed. She's defeated. She can't stand it that her husband has pointed out someone else's happiness. Most people are like her, unable to be truly happy for those who have that which they themselves do not. In turn, they do one of two things: they either latch on with all they've got (take Josie for example), or they do their damnedest to avoid it all together. Tonight, it appears, we're caught up in the latching-on scenario. But this is mostly thanks to the overflow of alcohol that's being consumed. I look around and I wonder how we ended up here, in this ballroom, seated at a black-tie wedding with 398 of the lucky couple's closest friends (that's sarcasm) discussing topics we don't really care about— breaking bread with people we might like to kill, given the chance.

I try really hard for you, I do. Eventually though, it wears on me, and I can't take it anymore, all of this togetherness with people I don't really like, and I know it's time for a change. "He's here," I whisper, leaning in close. As I pull back, I study your face. You furrow your brow and then you narrow your gaze, and it pleases me. This expression means I've managed to surprise you. Although, it suddenly becomes clear, that maybe I'm mistaken. I'm not sure whether to be annoyed or elated that, unlike the rest of the people in this room, you get me, and even though it's getting harder and harder to impress you these days, I'll never stop trying, and maybe *that's* the secret.

"Ah," you say as realization sinks in. I'm giving you a wedding gift— only it's not our wedding. You lean in, and we're so close I can feel your lips brush my skin as you speak. "Why *here?*"

I shrug and study your face. "It's easy," I answer, and this is our brand of foreplay, this color-coded speak.

You cock your head to the side, press your lips together tight, and then you smile. "You've never been one for that."

"You're right," I tell you, and I'll give you that, even if it's not exactly true.

You look away, toward the dance floor, and then back at me. "Did you bring the stuff?"

"Of course," I tell you. You're always concerned about

the drugs, about my sources, and I've never let you down before so I'm not sure why you think I'm going to now. I wait to see if you have any other ridiculous questions, and when it appears you don't, I turn and ask our guests to excuse us. I say we need to phone the sitter. They watch as I stand and make a gesture for your hand. The women swoon, and I love that you love the attention. Always one to go the extra mile, I bring the inside of your wrist to my mouth and kiss it softly. I linger a second too long, I can tell by the way you sigh. As we turn you slip your hand in mine. We walk away, heads held high, the earth spinning under our feet. Eventually, I pass off the syringe and we're magic, you and me.

It's not all flawless though, because as we exit the ball-room you pause and you turn to me. "Are you really going to let me do the honors?" you ask and it's a dumb question, seeing that I've just handed you the syringe, but obviously this is how you're going to play it. It wouldn't have been my first choice, but I guess role-play isn't an exact science.

I raise my brow and offer a slight smile. "Happy birthday."

You narrow your eyes and then you study my face, and yes, we are playing the same game, the two of us. "My birthday is next month," you say.

"I'm aware," I tell you. "Happy early birthday."

"You're giving me a man's life?" you ask, and I don't know if it's meant to be a question but your voice is a few octaves too high and stupid never did suit you. "Don't you think that's a bit extreme?"

"Is there something else you wanted?"

"I can think of a thing or two," you say, and you wink. You're practically purring. You enjoy it when I play your games. I can tell by the way you seal the deal when you reach for my hand, only to grab my cock instead. You're a bad girl, you are.

"What'd he do?" you press, and this is more in line with the Kate I know. You like justice, too.

"Wife beater," I say. "Also, he has a thing for escorts."

"Escorts?"

"Escorts." I confirm. "That's how I got him here…"

You glance at the syringe, and I can tell by the way your face falls that you're disappointed. I expected as much, but that doesn't mean I hate it any less. You tilt your head, and then you eye me suspiciously, relentless as you are. "We couldn't do better than this?"

"Our entire neighborhood is downstairs…"

You twist your mouth. "So?"

"So— this is the safest way. Easy in and easy out—you know the rules."

You consider what I've just said for a moment and then you grin. "Yeah, well, that doesn't mean I have to like them."

It feels like you're in my head and we're good together, and weddings have a nostalgic effect on me, even if I hate them. I watch as you tighten your grip on the syringe and I'm relieved you've showed up as 'agreeable Kate' tonight. You meet my eye once again, sizing me up.

Leaders lead, and that's what you want—or rather that's what you need— and so I take your hand and I lead you toward the elevator. We ride up in silence because we know not everything needs to be said. I stare at you while you stare at the floor, and I wish I could crawl inside that crazy little head of yours and see what you're thinking. That's how I know we've still got it. I'd give anything to see your brain from the inside. I'd like to hold it in my hands, inspect its folds, dig around a bit. It's dangerous though, knowing a person this way. Where's the bottom, is there an end? I'm not sure, but I think the moment I figure you out, is the moment it's over.

You can see that I'm pensive, and I can see that you want

to know what I'm thinking. But mystery is healthy in a marriage, and that's all you need to know. When the doors open, I motion for you to exit, and as you do, my hand grazes your lower back. You lean into me, and as a reminder not to get too comfortable, I surprise you by swatting your ass. It causes you to jump, and you trip on your heel a little. I grab your elbow, steadying you, letting you know who's in charge, confirming that I have you and always will. "This way," I say and you smile and we walk silently, hand-in-hand to our room. To the outside world we look like lovers slipping off to a quiet place. And we are that, but we're more, too. You look up at me and you laugh, you little mind reader, you. You don't take your eyes off me as I place the key card in the door. We slip in, and I love seeing you this happy.

As you go around inspecting the room, you eye the items I've laid out, and you seem pleased. I can't help but notice you haven't slipped out of those heels, and I wonder if you know how much I like it this way.

"So you wanna fuck first?" you ask in your nonchalant way, and you look at me as you speak, your eyes lingering on every word.

"Let's do it after," I say, taking off my jacket. I feel your eyes on me as I unbutton my cuff links and roll my sleeves up, and it amazes me how so much can go without saying between two people and yet still be understood. *Maybe that's the secret.* But in this moment, I don't know what you're thinking, which both terrifies and excites me.

"Haven't you heard?" you ask, picking up the gloves I've left for you on the table. You slip them on.

"Heard?" I ask, doing the same with mine.

You don't answer immediately. Sometimes you tell and sometimes you show, and in this case you saunter over and stand before me. You show me you're ready by loosening my bowtie. "It's always better to get the hard stuff out of the way first," you say, and you slur a little as the words roll off your tongue. You've transformed into sexy, sultry Kate, and you know how much I like it when she comes out to play.

"Then we'd better get to it," I offer, stepping away from you. Not because I want to—but because it's up to me to keep us on task, and also because I haven't considered that you might be tipsy.

"You're the boss," you sigh and then for good measure you salute me like the asshole you are, and although you sound drunk I don't think much of it, probably because you're a smart ass all the time. Maybe though, if I'd listened, things might have gone differently. "You're the boss," you say again just to drill it in, and it takes me back.

～

I AM A KID AGAIN IN THAT ALL TOO FAMILIAR BAR, STICKING out like a sore thumb, and yet not knowing anything different. It smells of cigarettes and cedar and dying dreams, and even though I'm young, I know that whatever my future holds, it isn't this.

"You're the boss," my mother says to my father. She has her head thrown back and she's laughing hysterically, and even though I hate this place, I have to admit that it's kind of nice seeing her this happy.

"Grab the door, Jude," my father orders, and I move quickly, doing as he says. Everyone stares, although I'm not sure why. This isn't the first time they've witnessed what comes next.

"I asked you not to serve her," my father says to Joe, the bartender. His tone is harsh. My father is angry, which doesn't happen often, and it's poor Joe that seems to take the brunt of it. Which is too bad, because I like Joe. He always gives me free soda. My father says we don't take free stuff, and that Joe is a loser just out to make a buck off of people who can't help themselves.

"I'm sorry, man. She doesn't let up."

"That's the problem," my father says, shaking his head.

He turns to my mother then, who has laid her head on the bar, and I watch as he lifts her off the barstool and takes her into his arms. He makes it look so easy. But she's thin now, thinner than I've ever seen her. Likely on account of the alcohol, but also because these days she rarely eats.

"I told you," she says staring up at my father. "SEE! Didn't I tell you all?" She huffs and she slurs as she addresses her audience, the fellow bar patrons. "He worries too much..." she offers, and then she laughs and looks directly at me. I don't know if it's intentional or because she's worried that I'm about to hear what she's about to say—that's the thing with my mother, you never knew. "I've told him and I've told him," she laments, throwing her hands in the air. "That everything bad that could happen already has."

∽

"Okay," you say. "I'm ready."

"It's about time," I tell you, doing my best to shake old memories from the corners of my mind.

It's pitch black when I slip into the adjoining hotel room, which is nice because it helps me focus on the present, on the here and now. I had been worried that the mark would check the lock on the door, the way any smart person would. But, it appears he isn't that smart; he hasn't checked and the door that connects our rooms remains unlocked. I motion for you to join me and then I reach for you in the dark. You bump into me. You're fumbling, and this should be my second clue that the champagne was a bad idea. I can't help but be irritated with you. It's showtime, and you're acting like a novice.

You think it was easy setting this all up? No, it wasn't. The planning, the fact that we managed to score an adjoining room, these things don't just happen, Kate. I make them happen— and look at you taking it all for granted, doing your best to fuck this up. I grab your wrist and step backward into our room, quietly pulling the door closed behind me. I give you a once over, which I'm pretty sure you can just barely make out. "Wait…" you whisper. "I forgot the syringe…"

In this moment, I could kill you. I massage my temples instead. We look like the most inept assassins on the planet and why did I ever think this was a good idea? We don't work well together. Not when it comes to murder. Also, you were right, I realize that now. We should have fucked first. Things tend to run smoother that way.

"Just kidding," you laugh, and you grab my ass, and this is the third clue I mostly ignore. Your head isn't in the game, and therefore I know I'm going to have to work double-time. Once to cover your ass, and once to cover mine.

For a second, I consider calling it. Or at the very least explaining it all again, especially given your level of distraction, but we've already run through the game plan twice and now it's go time. "You want me right outside the bathroom, right?" you ask. You're chewing at the side of your cheek, staring at me with those doe eyes that I find hard to resist, and it isn't like you to be this unsure.

I give you a look because I don't understand the confusion, and then I shake my head and I wonder where I went wrong.

I run through it again. "We spent ten minutes, at least, watching the cameras I placed," I tell you. "We have a visual of our target entering the shower, which means there isn't time to stand here and have a fucking powwow. Get in. Get out. That's how this goes."

"Right," you say and you leave it at that.

Now is not the time for a fight. "The camera's...um..."

I check my watch. "We have to do this now," I tell you. You can see that I'm going in with or without you. You look back at the TV screen and then at me, and I must be missing something. You watched particularly closely, so why you're confused now escapes me. He's not exactly what you'd call unattractive, which irritates me further— guys like him always get away with more than they should, and then there's the fact that he's naked. Yes, I saw you gawking, and maybe this has something to do with why you don't seem to know what the fuck is going on. We can go from zero to sixty in no time flat, you and I, and your only saving grace is that he's going to be dead in a matter of minutes.

"Let's try this again," I say before I open the door slowly. You follow me inside where we wait. In the soft yellow light, I can see the impatience on your face, and not once do you take your eyes off mine, not even when you should.

I know you know the plan, we've been over it, and so why you deviate from it is beyond me. You were supposed to wait for him to exit the bathroom, subdue him, and inject him with the drugs. It is supposed to be fairly straightforward. Simple. But then, nothing with you ever is, and as it all goes down, you react several milliseconds too slow. He senses you before he sees you, and he reacts by grabbing you by the neck. He pins you to the wall. And this guy, he's big. He's into mixed martial arts, and you'll later argue this is the part I've failed to mention. Luckily for you, it bothers me that he has my wife in a chokehold, and that he's not wearing any clothes. My only relief is how pissed you look. You make the wrong move and you take an elbow to the left eye, but it's me who feels the blow hardest. I can't help but look on, vying for you, silently. *Go for his eyes.* Only you don't do what I want. In fact, you do the exact opposite when you knee him in the groin, and why is this always a woman's signature move? It barely fazes him, and this is when I realize I have to step in. Sliding the extra syringe from my pocket, I remove the cap. Had you known I was prepared to come to your rescue, you would've said it was unnecessary. Thankfully for the both of us, I keep a few things to myself and I ignore your nonsense. You're lucky I'm always three steps ahead.

I take a step forward and position myself. You're doing your best to fight back, and so I give you a second, just to see if you can pull it off, but this guy he has experience manhandling women and I know you can't. I count to three and on two I step out from the shadow and jam the needle into his neck. He staggers backward, pauses, and then he lunges. I'm quicker though, I've anticipated it, and I move away. It takes him a few seconds to fall but eventually he does, and the thud with which he hits the floor is louder than I would've liked. You slip forward, away from the wall he had you against, and you're panting. You move to kick him, but I stop you by grabbing you by the waist from behind. I lift you slightly off the ground, while you buck against me, and I want to ask where this energy was a minute ago, but then I don't want to beat a dead horse. You take losing hard, you always have. "No injuries," I say instead, and eventually you stop fighting me. I let you loose slowly. "Remember, Kate," I warn. "This is supposed to look like suicide."

"Whose?" you hiss, and then you brush by me in one of your rages. You don't give me time to tell you that your anger is misplaced, that all I did was help you out. You're a sore loser Kate, and sure, maybe I should have let you win— but that's okay because now we'll have to fuck it out. I would have told you this too, had you not huffed and puffed and exited the room, therefore forfeiting the game. You should know better. Quitters never win.

DEAD IN THE WATER

CHAPTER THREE

KATE

I t takes you a while over there, and it kills me to have walked out of that room. You know I've always liked the staging part. Which is why it takes everything in me not to go back and finish this fight, but I won't give you the satisfaction. I have staying power, and so instead I pour myself a drink and I pace. I will wait you out. That much I can do.

Finally, when I hear you making your way through the door, I stop pacing. You stand there, removing your gloves, wiping the sweat from your brow, and it's a dig at me, the kind you offer best without words. You watch me as I down the last of my drink and then you pour yourself one I doubt you'll really drink.

"Cheers," I offer, but it sounds like 'fuck you,' which it is, and I hate that we haven't touched glasses. It's bad luck, and certainly we don't need any of that. You don't seem concerned with luck though, because in two short strides you are standing in front of me, and your eyes are dark. You swallow hard, and this intensity, it kills me. You don't say anything, and I hate the silence between us. Maybe you're trying to send a message. Maybe you're into telepathy; I'm not sure. But I'm not afraid of this side of you, Jude. It's always been the best part. And so when you push me against the wall, I go willingly. At least at first. Because I know you, and you've always enjoyed a bit of a fight.

I want to be mad, but it's hard when you look at me like that. This is why I hold my breath as you run your hands up the length of my sides and back down again. I won't give in; I won't give you the satisfaction. Until I start to feel dizzy, and then I sigh and let it out. You want submissive, fine. I'll give it to you. I'm tipsy and I'm angry and I don't want to waste this. I look you directly in the eyes, and for the first time it feels like you're actually seeing me. I guess the allure of sex does that to a person.

"Ouch," you say, touching my swollen face, taking me by the chin, pulling me toward the light. "We need to get some ice on that."

I don't give you the dignity of a response. Instead, I motion toward the bed. You glance over at my suggestion, but you don't budge, or at least not much, and so I nudge you in the direction I want you to go. Taking you by the shirt, I lead you over to the bed. You like what I'm thinking, and so you make it easy to get you where I want you. You smile as I push you down, and then you stare expectantly as I straddle you and unfasten your belt. You like control— but you like blow jobs better—and you need to be punished for setting me up next door the way you did.

Only now isn't the time for punishment— there will be other opportunities, and you should keep that in mind. I'm a woman, Jude, and with women, nothing goes unnoticed. I won't soon forget that I didn't get my kill tonight because you have some sick need to show me what a man you are, and even if I secretly kind of love it, I can't let you off the hook. *Give an inch, they take a mile. My father said that.* You're studying my face, and I can see that you want to know what I'm thinking but I won't let you in. Not that way.

By the time I step back and slide my dress over my hips, you're already hard.

"Come here," you say, and at first I don't, but then I do.

~

WHEN THEY ASK ME TO JOIN THEM IN THE LADIES ROOM, IT'S the first time I realize the severity of our situation. Maybe I should have seen this coming. But I didn't.

On our way back down to the reception, rounding the corner, we ran into Anne and I swear she knows. We couldn't hide the fact that our faces were flushed or that our clothes were a bit disheveled and thank god we fucked. At least there was that. The smell of sex tends to throw people off the scent of murder. Either that— or the two go hand-in-hand and sometimes it's hard to know. There was more afterward, where chemistry is concerned, only it's the kind that is manufactured and it's clear you're feeling that too.

"Oh my," she says and her hand goes straight to her surgically enhanced chest. Your eyes follow; you can't help yourself. You're practically drooling, and it's cute, but we both know it isn't because of her tits. "What happened to your eye?" she asks drawing out the words, letting them linger like her hand on those double Ds.

I jut my bottom lip out and press my finger to the bruise to show it's nothing. But it's not nothing, already it's turned an ugly shade of green that no amount of makeup could conceal completely. "Oh, this," I say, laughing, and I touch it once more even though it hurts like hell. "I wasn't watching where I was going, and well, these hotel doors, they don't mess around." You're still staring at her chest when I wave my hand in the air, doing my best to change the subject, simultaneously drawing her attention away from your poor manners. "It actually looks way worse than it is."

"Well," she says curtly, and she stands up a little taller, asserting herself. "Maybe all that champagne had a little something to do with it," she adds as though it's a question, when it isn't. She purses her lips and she doesn't hide the fact that she doesn't believe me about the door.

"Maybe," you pipe in and you slur a little. "But to tell you the truth, Annie," you say, and you lower your voice as though you're about to offer her the secret to the universe, and at this point, you're so high, maybe you are. Still, you know she hates it when people call her Annie, and why must you always go around offending my friends? "It's just—my wife likes it a little rough."

I almost roll my eyes, but I know how much Anne appreciates manners and we can't *both* fuck this up, so I manage a tight smile instead. Then I laugh you off. "I think it's my husband who has had a few too many," I confess, frowning for good measure, just so she sees my displeasure at your poor taste.

It works. Her expression is about as condemning as they come. Just to hammer it in, you lean in and you add fuel to the fire. "Yeah, and I intend to have a few more before it's all said and done…" you say to me and you laugh but you don't stop there. "Whatcha say Annie… you fancy a twirl across the dance floor?"

She politely and disapprovingly declines your offer, and then she informs us they're about to cut the cake.

"Let them eat cake," you exclaim, wielding an invisible sword directly at Anne's chest, and I swear to God, Jude, you're an expert at pissing people off. I can tell by the way she shakes her head and excuses herself—thankfully. Damn it, why must you always surprise me?

It's payback, I get it. You want me to be sorry. And I am

sorry for sticking that needle in you—I do know how much you hate them. But you're lucky, I know my limits. It's not so bad, at least now you're happy, and we aren't fighting, so there is that. Plus, I only injected you with a little— just enough to take the edge off—just enough so you learn your lesson and so Anne and now probably everyone else you come in contact with will think you've had a few too many. You're not much of a drinker, though, you never have been, which took getting you drunk off the table. Which meant that I was out of options if I wanted to get my way, so tell me, what was a girl to do?

It was imperative that I get back into that room and give that bastard what he deserved, and it was obvious you weren't going to let me at him willingly. And if I do say so myself, I think I did a bang-up job. I really gave it to him, a fact that redeems your previous behavior, your deception, your lack of sportsmanship—but only a little. You may have set me up to fail, you may have stolen my kill, but you certainly didn't get the last laugh, now did you?

Sure, you may be laughing now. Making a fool out of yourself and me as well, in front of our friends. But this is far from over. You didn't get the final say, and neither did he.

He didn't say much. You made sure of that. Still, I have a strong distaste for any man who hits women, and in turn I strangled him with the sheet until he was better than dead. You said I couldn't touch him—that I couldn't rough him up — but you were wrong. After what he did to me— after what he did to his wife— he deserved worse. The thing most people don't realize about attempting suicide is that, more often than not, people have to give it a few tries before they succeed. It's ugly and it's messy, and most often a job done in desperation. You can't tell me you're dumb enough not to know this, and for this reason alone I don't feel the least bit guilty about drugging you. Also, if you must know— it didn't matter that he was already dead when I did what I did. Okay, well, actually it did matter a little. What didn't matter so much was that he didn't feel it. I felt it, and sometimes that has to be enough.

~

YOU'RE THE LIFE OF THE PARTY, TAKING TURNS DANCING WITH any woman who will have you while I pretend not to care. But you know what? Fuck you. Because we're about to tango, Jude, and you ain't seen nothing yet. In fact, I'm buzzing in more ways than one, and now these women have insisted on a get-together in the ladies' room. It shows they're interested, and so even though I've never understood why women seem hell-bent on making the process of elimination a group affair, I go anyway. After all, new friends are hard to come by when you're neck-deep in children and murder, and society dictates that the more friends one has, the better.

It's not that I care about making new friends per se, but for the kids, I do what I have to do to fit in. Unfortunately for me, according to the internet, this means being chummy with the other moms. The thing is, I don't like being chummy, and I don't particularly like these moms. I don't tell *you* this, of course. But you probably know. And in any case, at least it provides a challenge. For instance, currently, it's a nice diversion from you and your sick need to win.

"Hey," one of them says, cornering me with her predatory smile. I think her name is Sharon. I'm pretty sure I've run into her at Bunko Night, which I quit going to because it never turned out well. I was damned if I do and damned if I don't. You know me, I don't like to lose, and they didn't like it when I always won. But I'm not willing to be a loser—so in the end I said fuck it.

Anyway, immediately I can tell that this Sharon lady, she's

out for blood. I recall beating her a time or two, and she doesn't seem like the kind who likes to be beat. "So..." she says, and she lowers her voice, going for the hushed tone effect, but it doesn't quite pan out that way. "I hope you don't mind... but I just have to know... how often do you guys..." she asks, looking away and then back at me. She lowers her voice further, so much that I can barely make out her words even though I already know what she is going to ask. "How often do you, um...you know?"

I cock my head to one side and smile sweetly. "Fuck?" I reply, hitting the nail on its head. Aside from the occasional run-in at Bunko, I haven't known most of these women long. They're friends of the bride and groom, who we also don't really know even though they live just down the street. It's not that I've tried to be antisocial, it's just that I've been busy getting my hands dirty. However, I've been told that if luck has it, our kids will be in preschool together. I wonder if it's such a bad thing to want to be unlucky?

They each giggle at either the 'F-word' or at my bluntness, likely both, and it's all the same. I've made them uncomfortable, but why skirt around the issue? They glance around at one another, hoping someone will say something to make the uneasiness go away. How old are we, I wonder? I don't say this, of course. Instead, I wait for one of them to come up with something better.

"Well, yeah... that," Claire says, finally.

I meet her gaze. "Usually, once a day," I offer with a shrug. "But sometimes... twice."

"No. Seriously?" Two or three of them utter in unison and I can tell they think I'm lying. But I can also tell there's a tiny part of them that believes I'm telling the truth, and this is what makes it hard to know which way to go.

"That's the truth," I assure them. I put my hands up in my

defense. They stare, their mouths gaping, and immediately I realize I should have taken the other route.

"Every day?" The one they refer to as 'June Bug' says. "Wow. That's crazy."

"It can be," I say.

"How do you find the time?" another asks. "I mean, *when* do you find the time?"

"She skips out at weddings—that's how," Anne interjects and I meet her eyes in the mirror. She's reapplying her lipstick, blindly, because she's glaring at me.

I shrug. It never occurred to me that people might actually want to know about our sex life. Not to mention the fact that I hadn't considered that they'd be this shocked by the answer. "We manage," I say, looking over at June and then I return Anne's gaze in the mirror. "And, yes, sometimes that means sneaking off for a few minutes to ourselves," I confirm with a smile and a nod.

They watch me closely. I wash my hands and dry them without a word. Eventually, I turn and address my audience. "But honestly, that's about as much as I want to say about it," I admit, checking my reflection in the mirror. They seem confused at my bluntness, and so I eye them curiously. "I guess I just haven't figured out how it's anyone's business," I conclude, focusing my gaze on Anne once again. She doesn't meet my eye, and I realize that while Sharon might be out for blood, it's Anne who's the dangerous one.

It gets awkward quickly, so I tell them I'd better get back. I dry my hands a second time and I'm awfully confused by this turn of events. When did a little mystery stop being a good thing?

I exit the restroom, but it instantly feels like the wrong thing to have done, so I pause outside the door in an attempt to catch my breath and figure out how things went so very wrong in there. I was supposed to come out better off than I went in. Instead, I'm worse for the wear, not to mention empty-handed.

Anne exits the bathroom, and I pretend to be staring at my phone. As she passes, she hesitates. "That, husband of yours," she says, turning on her heel. She offers a tight smile and then she exhales slowly. "He really is some dancer."

"Yes," I say. "He is." I won't let her get me, I won't.

"Maybe I'll have to take him up on that offer after all."

I smile, and I hate trying to be normal when it would be so easy just to kill her instead.

⁓

I DON'T GO BACK INTO THE BALLROOM. NOT IMMEDIATELY. AS I stand there trying to collect myself, I realize the mistake I made with those women. *If luck has it...our kids will have the same teachers!* The memory hits me like the scent of garbage on a hot day.

"Spit on her," I hear them chant. I am transported back to third grade, and I'm on the ground in the duck and cover position. I squeeze my eyes shut, hoping it'll be over sooner than the last time. Someone kicks me hard in the ribs and I feel wetness running down my leg. It stings my skin, but it could be the fire ants again. That's what got me last time. Hundreds of fire ant bites kept me out of school for a week. The punishment was being at home, locked in my room, for not fighting back. I tried though, I did. It's hard to even the playing field when it's seven against one. "Do it already," a boy orders. "Hurry up loser, Mrs. Smith is coming!" another voice says.

This is the third time this week that they've cornered me on the playground, the third time I've been in the fetal position, and it's only Thursday. Yesterday it rained, and so we had recess inside, but it didn't matter, they always find their ways. Someone dumped all the stuff out of my desk and Sarah stabbed me with her pencil 'on accident.' On the bus, they made me sit on the floor. It wasn't so bad. At least then the bus driver could see when they pulled my hair.

But today takes the cake. Today, I had to pee. Only I held it because I'm tired of being followed into the restroom. Boys are pretty hands on with their measures, but girls, they use words too. Mostly, they just call me names, but sometimes they pull my hair, and other times it's just a shove here and there. Oddly enough, it's the names that hurt the worst, the latest of them being 'rat girl.' This one seems to have stuck. They tell me I'm dirty, and they aren't exactly wrong. Sometimes when my mother forgets to wash, I come to school in clothes I've already worn. But it's not because I want to stink, and it's not because I'm lazy. It's because my father won't allow me to use the washing machine. He says we all have to suffer for my mother's 'ineptitude' —whatever that means— otherwise she'll never learn. Today it sucks more than most days, the name calling and the spitting, because I spent three hours yesterday washing my clothes by hand in an attempt to get the stink out. They were still damp when I put them on this morning, but at least they didn't smell as bad. In addition, I missed my homework, and Mrs. Smith put a note in my folder, and I know what that means when it comes to my father. Basically, it means I'm screwed, and I won't get dinner or a shower tonight. These things have to be earned, he says.

It all seems rather hopeless, now, as I'm lying on the ground. A hint of sunlight peeks through the fingers I use to shield my face, and maybe I can do extra chores. I hope that works because today I'm hungrier than usual. I didn't get to eat lunch because Jimmy poured his milk all over my tray. The truth is, I was hungry enough to eat it, it's my pride that wouldn't let me.

Maybe that makes them right about me, I don't know.

"Rat girl, rat girl," they sing. "Watch out or she'll get you. And then you'll stink too."

I lay there and I study the sliver of light coming through my fingers, and I know it'll be over soon. I can feel myself being covered in spit, and maybe it's the kicking, and the jarring, or the fact that I'm distracted by the light, because I surely don't mean to, but I can't help it. I wet myself. It isn't a trickle. It's everything I couldn't hold back.

"I just couldn't hold it any longer," I tell my mother when she comes to the office to pick me up.

"For God's sake, Lydia. You're eight years old."

"I'm sorry," I say. "Do you think you'll be able to get to laundry tonight? They spit on me."

"Why would they do such a thing?"

I shrug and she looks at me as though I'm the one that's lost my mind. "They say our family is weird…"

"Hmmm," she says and I'm not sure she's really listening to me. She does that sometimes; she's good at tuning out what she doesn't want to hear. These days it's becoming more and more.

"I could do the laundry," I tell her, my voice full of hope. "And tell Dad you did it."

"We'll see," she says and she grips the steering wheel. Then she turns to me and her expression is stone cold. "But you know your father. He knows everything."

"I have pee on me…and he took the rest of my clothes…"

"Yes," she says. "But you deserved it," she concludes, and I know how much she hates driving, how much she despises leaving the house. I can see it in the way she looks at me.

"I'm sorry," I say again, if for no other reason than to fill the silence.

"I know," she tells me. "But damn it, Lydia. Can't you try just a little harder to fit in?"

~

THINKING OF OUR CHILDREN, SUDDENLY I REALIZE I HAVE TO fix this. I can't alienate them the way I've alienated myself—it's not their fault their mother doesn't know how to solve problems without drawing blood. Despite what you think, I realize I should probably be more relatable. I'm just not very good at these things. But you're dancing, and so I figure now seems like as good a time as any to practice.

As I push the door open, ready to tell them that I was only kidding, ready to concede to them asking about all of the nitty-gritty details of our personal life, ready to be as creative as ever in my answers— even though I couldn't care less about conversing with these women, I am thankful to see that they've dispersed into the stalls and that maybe I won't have to.

"Personally, I think she's lying," I hear one of them say and while I'm not certain, it sounds like Sharon.

"I think they're weird. You know— like...sex addicts or something.... I mean *who* has sex *every* day?"

"I don't know," one of them replies. "But have you seen the way he looks at her? I think she's telling the truth."

They sigh in unison.

"Maybe," Sharon says, and this time I know for sure it's her by her inflection, and by the way she pauses, mostly for effect. It's obvious she's the ringleader, and my biggest obstacle if I want our children to have any friends. "But I still think they're weird."

~

CHAPTER FOUR

JUDE

I don't remember most of last night. *But then, I wouldn't, would I?*

It's still dark out, just before dawn, when I wake, naked, with full-on cottonmouth and a headache that feels like it might do me in. You're wrapped up in a sheet, peaceful, and I let you sleep even though I consider killing you now and getting it over with.

Even though my memory is hazy, I know that whatever happened won't have been good, and taking you out now will save us some time arguing later. It's astonishing—just think, I could save us years of back and forth with one swift movement. It takes me a moment to reconsider, and it's helpful that I can just barely make out your right tit peeking out, but eventually I decide where's the fun in that? So, I take a cold shower instead, and then I dress quietly and head downstairs in search of aspirin and coffee.

Part of me wants to wake you, just to be mean, but I let you sleep because I'm not ready for your wrath, not yet. There's a storm brewing between us, and in times like these it's helpful to have a plan. Mostly though, I've learned—especially where you're concerned— that not reacting is often the best action.

I make my way downstairs, only to find that the lobby is deserted. It's my favorite time of day, before all the hustle, when things are still, quiet, as they should be. I sit, reading the paper, or trying to. I can hardly think, my head is throbbing so badly, but I still manage to finish off my coffee.

I can't say I noticed anything out of the ordinary.

But then, I wasn't really looking.

~

"You weren't looking," my father says.

"I was looking," I swear.

I'm six, and it's my first time hunting. I don't shoot the doe, not because I wasn't looking, but because I don't want to.

"Then why did you miss the shot?"

I shake my head. "I just don't see the point of this..."

"Does there need to be a point in order for you to do what you're told?"

I shrug. I'm being particularly petulant this morning because I'm angry at my father for having been away so much recently. This is my way of punishing him, mostly because I don't have the words to verbalize it. And also, there's a part of me who isn't sure if it's my anger or if it's my mother's that I've brought with me to this cold, gray field he has us set up in.

"What if that deer were going to kill you or someone you loved," he says raising his brow. "Then would you shoot it?"

"A deer can't kill people."

"Sure it can. Happens all the time on the highway. They jump right out in front of cars—sometimes taking out entire families."

I refuse to look at him. I know how much he hates that. "I just don't like hunting. "

"Well, look," he says, his tone neutral. I hate it that he refuses to give in. He refuses the bait. "Your mother says I have to bring you. Plus, I'm not raising a pussy. So shoot the fucking deer and get on with it. You're not that special, Jude. You don't get to pick and choose what you want to do based on what you like. Sometimes, you have to do what you have to do, for no other reason than it needs to be done."

"I don't want to shoot the deer," I tell him.

He takes his rifle and lays it on the ground and then he does the same with mine. He commands my attention in the way that only he can. "I'm sorry I've been gone so much," he tells me, looking me square in the eye. "I know it's hard on you. But there's a man out there, a bad man, and he had to be dealt with. And here's the thing son: there are a lot of bad men, women too, that no one wants to deal with. So they get away with their crimes until someone decides to do something about it. In this case, this man was hurting children. Children like you. Which is another reason I brought you—I need to know that if I'm not around...and we both know I haven't been—I need to know that you can take care of yourself."

"How is shooting a deer going to prove that?"

"It proves that you can do things you don't want to do. And that's the important part, Jude."

I swallow and I exhale, long and slow. Then I pick up the gun and I wait for the next deer to come along, and when it does I take my shot. I understand what my father was trying to say. He is sorry for being away so much but he has to do what he has to do. I am sorry for all of us. The deer included.

～

BACK IN THE HOTEL ROOM, YOU SLEEP WHILE I PACK UP MY things. I don't take care to mask the noise, but you don't seem to mind. You'll be up any minute now, and this means it's time to go and check on our guy before I have to deal with you and before you have time to get any other crazy ideas. I can't remember much of what happened after I killed him, but if I know you—and I do—I know it won't have ended there. I don't want to go back in that room— it's risky being this close, and I don't particularly care for corpses— but I need to survey the damage and so I do what I have to do. One thing is for sure— this is the last time I'll offer you a kill; you've officially lost the right to my generosity. Worst of all, I want to be pissed at you, but it's hard to pinpoint exactly where to start when I can't recall why I'm feeling so uneasy or what it is you've done *this* time. Aside from injecting illegal substances into my bloodstream, that is.

One would think that would be enough.

But with you, nothing ever is.

WHEN YOU FINALLY CRAWL OUT OF BED AND SHAKE THE SLEEP off, you don't speak to me, you head for the shower instead. I almost join you, I figure we can settle this there, the way we do best, but we're short on time. Olivia's birthday party is this afternoon and you've invited forty people who aren't really our friends to come over and why we have to have such elaborate affairs I'll never understand. You say we need friends, for the kids, but in my experience friends only add another layer of complexity—to an already complicated life. They add problems we don't need. Like birthday parties for example. We don't need those either. The kids won't miss what they don't know. I even go so far as to tell you that I never had them, and I turned out fine. But you apparently disagree, and I lost that battle. Not to worry, I haven't lost the war.

Speaking of war, I grab my gun and cock it before unlocking and opening the door to the adjoining room. As I step inside, the silence is deafening. It's clear there's nothing alive in this room. Making my way over to the bed, I see that not only is something very, very wrong, but it's worse than I expected.

He's dead, obviously, but also worse for the wear, and what the fuck have you done, Kate?

My throat clenches shut as I survey the damage.

It isn't pretty. But more so, there's something off, something odd. In his mouth is crumpled up paper.

I reach down and try to remove it, but rigor mortis has set in, and I have to pry his jaw open to pry it loose, which takes some effort. Once I'm able to get his mouth open, it takes some digging and fishing around to remove the paper, but once I manage to get it all out, I find it's a note—typed out.

I've got my eye on you.

~

WE CHECK OUT OF THE HOTEL, AND NO ONE ASKS QUESTIONS. Meanwhile, I'm just waiting for it. Even though I've paid in cash and used an alias, your favorite John Water, I'm half-expecting someone or something to call us out, to pull us to the side, to stop us and ask us about the mark. Maybe they'll ask if we saw anything strange, and we did. Or maybe they'll accuse us of murder, and they won't be wrong. I may not look worried from the outside. It's an art I perfected ages ago. However, I'm dying a little inside. Suspense has never been my thing. But you, you're cool as a cucumber.

Which is why we argue all the way home. You say you

didn't write the note, and that while you roughed him up a bit, you are certain you did not type that out, and I don't know what to believe. Maybe you had so much to drink that you just don't remember. I tell you this, and you bring up the fact that I danced with other women. Give me a fucking break, Kate. Not only do those women not hold a candle to you, I did it for you. Because it's what you want. You want us to make friends. You want us to fit in with these people—or at least you say you do—but then you say a lot of things, and at this point I'm not sure what to believe.

I tell you this and we go 'round and 'round until we're in the driveway and we have to go in, and for fuck's sake Kate, this is a nightmare. Dead guys do not write notes to their killers. I just need to know how this happened, and either you don't know— or you won't tell me— and I haven't got time for surprises. "So which is it?" I demand, giving you one last shot at truth.

"I don't know what you want from me," you reply. I'm not surprised.

You can't say.

Instead, you assure me it's all going to be fine.

But this isn't the time for predictions, and how can you know?

≈

I SWEAR YOU'RE LIKE A WILDFIRE I CAN'T CONTAIN. JUST WHEN I think I have you under control—you go another direction. I don't know how we got here, in this downward spiral, when just last night we were fine. But we're going downhill fast, and it seems nothing can save us now.

Currently, you're rushing around like a crazy person. Which you are. The fact that our guests are due to arrive any minute only confirms my suspicions about your sanity. Not to mention that you've reminded me of the time no fewer than a dozen times in the last half-hour alone.

This is your way of punishing me because I can't let it go. We've been over and over the details of last night, and still all you offer is silence. Also, I forgot to pick up the balloons. So now you're talking around me, in circles, just not *to* me, and your brand of punishment has always been an interesting one. Of course, you'll employ other tactics later, but not now, not so long as you need my help with your endless list of 'honey-do's.' So for now, you resort to the simple stuff—letting me know exactly how many minutes are left on the clock. But that's you. Always one to keep score.

"Do we really need them?" I inquire once more, and your expression lets me know how ridiculous a question you think this is. You won't dignify my apparent ignorance with an answer. Your long, drawn out, not the least bit dramatic sigh tells me what I need to know. The answer is yes. It's pretty clear by the way you roll your eyes that you think I'm incompetent. But you can't know that I didn't pick up the balloons because after I dropped you off, I had a job to do and nothing went as planned. You don't know that peoples' lives were on the line, namely my own, and you can't know how badly I needed to get this job right. It would not soothe you to hear that the last thing on my mind was two-dozen fucking balloons... but rather on that note you supposedly did not write and the paycheck that keeps us afloat.

I'm watching you now, and that's the thing, I'm always watching you until I'm not, and that's when we find ourselves in trouble. You throw up your hands and offer me another one of your looks. You want to know why I'm just standing here, and it isn't helping matters any that one of the kids has taken my keys and they are now God-knows-where.

To avoid another one of your looks, I call out to Monique, our nanny. She doesn't answer immediately. Of course, she doesn't. The clock is ticking, and you are unforgiving, and so I've decided I'll just take the car we've loaned her, but first I need the keys. You stop at the top of the stairs, look down at me and roll your eyes again, and I don't know how many of these bitchy looks you can throw out in a day, but I've about reached the quota of the number I'm willing to take. You think I'm going to ask her to pick up the balloons. But I won't, because I'm not you.

Also, I need to get out of here. I need to get away from this fiasco of a birthday party you've created. It's circus-themed because that's what Olivia requested and I can't help but wonder if you see the irony here.

I call for Monique again. I eye the top of the stairs and I wait. Eventually it's you who appears again and this time you're wearing a dress, which I can see straight up, and suddenly everything I've ever wanted is in full view.

I'd be willing to bet if we fucked I could let some of this animosity go. After all, there's nothing like the scent of sex to clear the air. But your resistance to the idea feels pretty palpable and also you'd argue we don't have time. And baby, that's all we've got. You waltz by, and damn, I like what I see — even though you really should wear panties. This is a children's party, for fuck's sake. You give me another look, and it's clear you've read my mind. I call for Monique again, but I already know that she isn't coming because I can hear that she's dealing with Brady. He doesn't like the outfit you've picked out for him, and he's refusing to put it on, and it's poor Monique who is getting the wrath. "You little rat," she tells him and I watch your face. You're easy to read when you don't think I'm looking, and you don't like it when she speaks to him that way.

I don't know what to tell you other than I've never understood why we 'need' a nanny in the first place. It's absurd if you ask me, having another adult here in our home, caring for our children, when we are two capable, able-bodied people. But absurdity matters little, I guess, when one is married to *you.*

You want what you want and somehow you always find a way to get it.

In this case, I came home one day to find a young girl all moved in. You introduced the two of us as though I were expecting her— as if I weren't the stranger in my own home.

You yell out the time again so rudely, interrupting my fond memories. Finally, Monique appears at the top of the stairs. Brady stands behind her, and I can tell he's been crying. He rarely cries, and I watch as you go to him. I think you should let him be, but I know you won't. I ask Monique for her keys, and I watch for a moment as she digs in her bag hurriedly. She's nervous, she's always nervous, but then, you have that effect on people. Even so, I don't know what to make of her; she never meets my eye and I find myself tiptoeing around her in my own home. Truthfully, I think she's onto you, but I can't say for sure. We barely speak the same language, and still I wouldn't bet against her knowing our secrets. Which is just the first of many reasons I don't want anyone in our home.

Clearly, opposites attract though, because you remind me yet again that half of our neighborhood is 'due to arrive any minute.' I watch on, half-amused, half-irritated, as you come around the side of her and bark orders at me like you've forgotten who I am. I mouth the words 'fuck you' and then I turn for the kitchen, thinking of a hundred and one ways I plan to punish you and your non-panty wearing self, just as soon as I can find the time. At the moment it has to wait, as duty calls, and apparently we can't have a party without balloons. It's actually those fucking balloons I'm thinking about when I hear the series of thuds. It's unmistakable, that sound, it's the kind of thud that can only mean one thing, and as I round the corner I pray it's not as bad as I think. I pray it's not one of the kids.

Thankfully, it isn't.

It's Monique, and she's lying at the bottom of the stairs.

She isn't moving.

You stare down at me, your mouth open, and for once there's nothing coming out.

∼

CHAPTER FIVE

KATE

Olivia is in her room when it happens. I've just looked in on her, in order to remind her for the umpteenth time to clean up the dresses she's left strewn about the floor. Instead, she taps on her iPad, headphones on, oblivious to me, oblivious to the world. She likes her clothes there, she's told me before. This way, she knows just where to find them, and how did I ever not for a moment think that our children would have personalities big enough to rival our own? It doesn't matter that she's not technically my flesh and blood. There's that whole nature versus nurture thing, and she's her father's daughter through and through. Every once in a while I catch a glimpse of myself in there, but mostly she's all you. This is what I'm thinking when I see the nanny tumbling down the stairs.

It all happens so fast, and before I know it I've got Brady by the shoulders and I'm ushering him in with his sister. "Monique fell down," he tells me as I slam the door and grab his iPad from the shelf. I shove it in his hands. "Yes. Stay here," I demand. Having lost privileges to his device over the past two weeks he seems more than happy to oblige, and although his reaction— or lack thereof— is concerning, right now it's the girl at the bottom of the stairs who needs my attention.

When I finally reach the bottom you are already kneeling over her. I lean in to get a better look, and immediately I know this isn't good. She isn't moving, and she isn't waking up, no matter what methods you employ to try to change the situation. I squint my eyes and concentrate hard on her chest in an attempt to see if I can see the rise and fall of it. I can't.

You check her pulse, again, and I watch as you press your lips together. You frown, and if I had to go on that alone I would know that our dilemma is not just bad, but very bad. Actually, it's even worse than you think. But you don't know that just yet.

Without hesitation you start CPR.

"Call an ambulance," you order, calling to me over your shoulder. I back away slowly and I chew on my lip until it bleeds and now I'm going to have to reapply my lipstick and who has time for that? You try to help her, and you give it your best shot, you really do. I know because it goes on forever. But I don't call for help as you've asked. Instead, I stand there mesmerized at your efforts and the blood, which slowly pours from her head onto my favorite rug. This is hopeless, I want to tell you, as you give it your all. Why can't you just call it? The doorbell is going to ring any minute and I'm guessing this is not the sort of sideshow our guests are expecting.

"How did this happen?" You demand to know, as you relentlessly pump her chest. Sweat has formed around your temples and I suddenly have the urge to reach out and touch you. I know better.

Instead, I watch as blood pools at the corner of her mouth

and I shrug. When I don't answer you look up at me and raise your brow. You don't look away, you wait until I'm forced to answer. "She was standing there one second... and the next she was tumbling down the stairs," I offer, knowing full well it won't be enough.

"We have to call 9-1-1," you say again. There's a part of you that knows this isn't possible, but there's the good part of you who wants to do the right thing and it's this I find most endearing. There's a battle brewing— always brewing— and it plays across your face. You're good at hiding most things, Jude. But never this.

"We can't," I tell you, finally.

You give me a look that lets me know you think I'm incredulous.

"And why is that?"

"I'm pretty sure she's illegal."

I watch as your expression changes. "So?"

"So we'll get in trouble. Plus, they might start asking questions..."

You shake your head, and begin pumping her chest again.

After several tries you look up again. "Remind me why we need a nanny?"

"Needed..." I say, nodding at her lifeless body.

Eventually, but not immediately after my comment, you decide to give up. Sheer willpower isn't going to bring her back to life, you realize, and so you push yourself up until you're standing and dust your hands off. You don't mean to do it, but body language is a funny thing, always telling, always giving our secrets away. You run your fingers through your hair. You're angry with me and close to losing it; I can tell by the way you massage your temples and drop your hands before resting them on your hips. You're contemplating what to do, and you know what needs to happen, even if you don't want to concede just yet. Unwilling to look at me, and give yourself away, you stare down at her, and I have to admit, the fact that you'd rather look at a dead girl hurts a little.

"We can't leave her here, Jude," I say, nudging you in the right direction. "The party starts in twenty minutes."

After several excruciating minutes of silence you shake your head. "Fine," you say. "Help me roll her up."

I do a double-take. "But that's my favorite rug."

You meet my eye and then tilt your head, and you look like you want to kill me, and I don't know how or why but right here in this moment I find you so very fuckable.

"Get over it," you say, and I like the edge in your voice. It's an inopportune time to be turned on, but what can I say? Sometimes these things just sneak up on you.

"Grab the end of the rug," you order. I like your intensity, so I do as I'm told, and I try to get over how much I love that rug. And I do.

Almost.

Nonetheless, I help you roll her up and then we haul her out into the garage and stuff her in your trunk. It's exhausting, and I can't remember the last time I did this much heavy lifting. That's what she was for.

∾

"I THINK I HEARD THE DOORBELL," I TELL YOU ONCE WE'VE made our way back into the house.

"We need to clean out the garage," you say, and I agree. Our situation gives *cleaning out the garage* a whole new meaning.

You sigh, and you're livid, and I have to tell you, it suits you. I can't make myself look away. You go to the sink and you wash your hands, and you don't look at me. You stare at the water as it runs red. Head wounds always bleed a lot, but you were careful and you're good with blood and dead girls and it's almost alarming, how adept you are at handling it all. The doorbell rings again, stealing my attention. "Perfect timing," you say in your best condescending tone. For good measure, and just to piss me off, you plaster a grin on your face even though I know you don't mean it at all.

"It's unfortunate you forgot those balloons," I tell you and you know exactly what I'm getting at when I say it. You know it isn't about the balloons at all. It's about the fact that the dead girl in the back of your car wouldn't be there had she not been standing at the top of the stairs digging in her bag— had you not called her there—had you done your job in the first place. It was so simple, too. Pick up a dozen balloons, save a life.

You don't reply, not immediately anyway, and so I turn and start for the front door. As I pass, you reach out and catch me by the forearm. You push me against the wall, pinning me there. You always did like my back against the wall. "Fuck you, Kate."

The doorbell rings again. "If only there were time," I tell you and then I slide out of your grip and shimmy away. I always did love a good party.

~

Josie and Sam are the first to arrive, as I knew they would be. "The kids are upstairs," I tell them knowing Brady will need a little coaching around what's just happened before I release him into the wild. "Jude's in the kitchen. If you'll go in and say hello, I'll go up and get them…"

I send Olivia down right away. It is her party, after all and to her nothing is out of the ordinary. I'll have to discuss the Monique situation with her later. I know Brady won't have said anything. It's rare that he speaks unless spoken to. But Brady, I hold back. He's changed out of the outfit he didn't want to wear and has managed to put on an old Halloween costume, which is exactly two sizes too small. I take his iPad away and grip him by the shoulders. "Brady," I say as his dark eyes bore into mine. He has your eyes. But it's my reflection I see in them. "Where is Monique?" I demand. I shake him a little even though I don't mean to.

He shrugs.

"When is the last time you saw her?" I ask.

He shrugs again.

"Monique got a job with another family." I tell him. "She is going to miss you very much," I add, knowing how important it is I get this right. "But there was another little boy... and well, he needed her more—because he's sick." He doesn't respond, and I wonder if he understands what I'm really saying, and it seems he does. Brady has always been exceptionally smart. He's different, and someday we'll need to address that, but today is not that day.

"I know," he tells me, looking away. "She has to take care of another little boy. Not Brady."

"That's right," I say, gripping his shoulders, wondering where he learned to speak of himself in third person. "That's exactly right."

"Don't worry, Mommy," he whispers, looking directly into my eyes, and it's as though he sees something there. Something that holds his attention. "I won't tell anybody," he promises, and I exhale for what feels like the first time all day.

"I'd hope not," I say, and then I sigh and pull him into my arms. As I pull back, I position him where I can see his face.

He doesn't cry. He doesn't look sad. In fact, I don't see any emotion at all.

"But I just have to know, Brady…"

He looks up at me and waits.

"Why did you push Monique?"

He hesitates, but only for a second, and then he shrugs slightly. "I didn't like those clothes."

~

CHAPTER SIX

JUDE

The road goes on forever and the party never ends. And I have to dispose of this dead girl before she starts decomposing, and we really should have thought this through a little better. This party is killing me slowly. It's a train wreck waiting to happen, and all I can do is look on in disbelief. I keep trying to figure out how to get all of these people out of my house. Like a fire drill or a stomach virus, or a dead body—you know, one of those things that instantly repels people. This is a crime scene, for heaven's sake, and kids are playing pin the tail on the donkey, because in whatever fictional world it is you live in says donkeys and circus themes and dead girls in the back of trunks go together. Here we are shooting the bull with our neighbors, laughing and chatting it up, and what would they say if they knew what we've just done? Do you think they'd let little Johnny stay for cake?

There's a reason you don't go inviting trouble into your house. Which is exactly what you have done. First with the nanny—and now with this party. And I can't help but consider that it was a mistake to think I could give you what you wanted—the house, the kids, the suburban dream—and still maintain any level of privacy. We live in a glass house, and all signs point to this being the way you want it. It's like you get off on living this close to the edge. Well, I hate to break it to you darling: we're not just living there— we're dangling by a thread.

"Where's Monique?" one of those Bunko ladies you constantly bitch about asks, and instantly I feel the thread shred just a little further. I think her name is Annie or something along those lines, but it's hard to tell. These women, they've always seemed one and the same to me. All I know is she's the one you like the least. She's the one who showed up at the hospital after, well, you know. Even then, I could tell she was the kind of person who likes to insert herself into horrible situations. She's an ambulance chaser, this one, keen to show what a good human being she is by taking any situation and finding the best way to make it about her. It's actually fairly impressive how good she is at it, too. I can see her now on the evening news, talking about the dead nanny she found in our garage, and how all along she just knew there was something off about us.

She isn't your friend, Kate. She burned you over that charity event, and she's pretentious and desperate at best. I've never quite figured out why you insist on being a part of this small cult of women. But you have a love/hate relationship with them beyond the scope of my understanding, and I don't get it, or at least that is what you tell me, word for word, whenever I ask why you hang around them if you despise them. The thing is, Kate, you think I don't get it—but I do. You're just too lazy to put in the effort to go out and find new friends. It's actually pretty simple, you just make it complex because you're a woman and because you enjoy the drama of it all.

"Well," you say, and now your face is twisting, but you don't dive in, not quite yet. You need all eyes on you, and you pause for full effect, always so theatrical. Eventually, my little drama queen, you speak. "It's just so hard to say out loud— I mean, it's like if I do…then I have to admit it's true."

"What?" Anne or Annie or 'whatever her name is' gasps. You get mad when I call her the wrong thing, but she's irrelevant, Kate, and that's why she tries so hard. She reaches out and grips your wrist to show how concerned she's pretending to be, when all she really wants is dirt she can use against you.

You inhale, and you glance briefly at the floor. You excel at deceit. "Monique quit this morning."

"No!" The women all say at once, and I could have predicted as much.

You fold your lips expertly and you wait. "I'm afraid so," you confirm after several nail-biting seconds. But you're smart, and you realize when to give them room to ask for more, and when to just get on with it. "She met someone online," you say, and you roll your eyes before breaking into a full grin, so clever you are. You like to mix it up. You look around and then you shake your head. "He lives in Ohio, apparently," you add, and you throw your hands up, dramatically. "I mean *who* lives in Ohio?"

The women sigh as though it's all so hopeless.

"Roughly twelve million people," I offer, always one to help, and almost in unison they turn and give me a look that only bitter women can give. It clearly says, 'Come on! Don't you see what we're up against here? The help has just left the building (actually she's in the trunk), and now we are at risk of having to lift one of our perfectly manicured fingers and figure shit out for ourselves.'

But not you. You don't give me that look. Your expression says something else entirely, something sinister, and for the first time today— maybe the first time this whole week— I remember exactly why I married you.

~

MY PHONE RINGS, AND YOU OFFER YOUR SIGNATURE LOOK OF disapproval, but it's a client. Which means it's a call I have to take. Turns out, it's my best client. I already know he's calling me out for a job—this one's urgent, but then they always are —and you will not understand that I have to go. As for the birthday girl, she could care less. She is happy and occupied with her friends, and I'm certain she won't even notice that I've slipped out before I'm back.

But you will, and if I know anything, it's that you'll never in a million years let me forget about it.

The thing about that is— you like this house, and the new SUV you drive and all of your earthly possessions.

I've never faulted you for that. I'd give you the moon, if I could manage. But you can't have it all, Kate.

If you want what you want, fine. I'll find a way to give it to you.

But you can't pitch a fit whenever my means don't justify your fantasy.

Life isn't fair.

Some of us have to work for a living.

Some of us *want* to work for a living.

And some of us just want to sit back and enjoy the party.

~

"JUDE," MY MOTHER CALLS, NUDGING ME AWAKE. I TURN TO her sleepily and I open my eyes to find that it's pitch black in my bedroom. "Jude," she says again and I can smell the liquor on her breath.

"Is everything okay?" I ask, sitting up, rubbing the sleep from my eyes.

"No," she says, a lisp to her voice that only manifests when she drinks. "Nothing is all right."

A lump forms in my throat.

"Your father called. He isn't going to make it back in time for my birthday...he said something about a snow storm or something—but you know how it is... it's always something."

"What time is it?"

She pauses and I hear the annoyance in her tone when she replies. My question wasn't what she expected. "Just after two."

I do the math. If she'll let me go back to sleep soon I can still get three hours in and then maybe I won't fall asleep in class and wind up with another detention slip.

"I'm sorry, mom," I say. "But we'll do something fun... I'll make you a cake."

"I don't want cake, Jude," she slurs. "What I want is a man who respects me."

"I know mom," I tell her. I quit standing up for my father a long time ago.

She sighs. "Then why would you suggest cake?" she asks and her voice grows louder and louder with each word. "Cake makes you fat. Men don't like fat women."

"You're not fat, mom."

She stands up, and I can see her shadow make its way around the room. I pray she doesn't start throwing stuff again. She picks up my old baseball trophy and studies it. "Well, I would be if I listened to you."

"It was just an idea."

"You know, it's sad...they give trophies to anyone these days. When I was a kid, people actually had to earn things— now people just make excuses and expect everything to be given to them."

"I'm sorry dad has to work," I say, letting her know I'm on her side.

"It's my BIRTHDAY. I just want a party. I don't see how that's too much to ask."

I sigh, realizing, there's no point in hope. I won't get to sleep anytime soon. I close my eyes and listen to her stumble around my room, fumbling in the dark.

"Listen," she says eventually. "I've been doing some thinking…your father will be back in the morning. Do you think you're old enough to stay alone for a few hours?"

"I'm seven," I tell her, and this time it's her turn to do the math.

"Yes, I know," she says laughing. "You're growing up…and someday you'll be gone…just like your father… and what about me? I'll be all alone… I'll have nothing."

I hold my breath, as she lifts the covers off of me and shakes them out. I'm afraid that she's going to order me out of bed. Sometimes, she wants to dance. Her mood seems too low for that now, but you never know. Finally, she tucks me in and I exhale. She pats the covers around my shoulders, making sure they're snug. "You'll need to get yourself off to school…"

I get myself off to school every morning, I think. But I don't dare say it aloud. I've learned to choose my words carefully. Even more so, when she's been drinking. It's not that I'm afraid of her. It just makes life easier.

"You're not going to drive, are you?" I ask cautiously.

She stands and she laughs. "Don't be so dramatic, Jude, darling. Of course, I am."

"But—"

She scoffs. "I'm getting older, you know. And, like they say, you only live once."

I don't know who they are, or who says that. But whoever it is, I hate them.

"Don't tell your father," she tells me as she closes the door, and I don't, because he doesn't come home for three days and neither does she.

~

CHAPTER SEVEN

KATE

You kiss my cheek and then you slip out, mostly unnoticed. But not by me. You're up to something. I think it's about that note, although I can't say for sure. You want me to tell you I wrote it, but the truth is, I can't. And now we have this situation with the dead girl in the back of your trunk, and these people in our house, and I want to follow you but you and I both know that I can't leave the party. You've trapped me this way; you've always been good at doing that. You say we don't need friends or birthday parties, but you can't very well pretend to be normal without the pretending part, Jude. This is where you're wrong. If we don't play their game, we're dead in the water. All animals have the ability to sniff out that which is not like them, and these people… they're dying to find the rat.

We either have to opt out all together or try to stay afloat. And it's sink or swim here in this place where everyone is all the same. Speaking of which, it doesn't help matters any that I'm standing here in our kitchen, surrounded by the same women who just last night said deplorable things about me. They think we're weird because we're happy. Maybe we were happier before we tried so hard to fit in, and I don't know why this is such a double-edged sword. But now they're here in my home, drinking my wine and eating my food, and pretending nothing was said, pretending nothing happened. I don't know how one is just supposed to simply forget the things they've heard—but I try my best. You're always telling me there's a time for revenge, and there's a time to lie in wait, and sometimes, believe it or not, I listen to you.

But that doesn't mean I enjoy them letting their kids run amok while they play nice, all the while knowing what they really think of me. That's also not to say I haven't weighed my options, I have. I could kill them all. But then we would have to move; we'd have to uproot the kids and now is simply not the time for the kind of work that would entail. Especially now that the help is dead. Plus, I really, really like this house. Which leaves me no choice—I have to make this work.

It does help some that Jane is here. She's always good at handling people. More than anything, Jane is good at mothering— which is ironic given that she technically isn't one. When you hired her all those years ago to stand in at our wedding, I never imagined that I might grow so fond of an actress, of all people. But she's good, and to tell you the truth, I've learned a thing or two from her. She comes in and she handles things. She collects her paycheck, and she never passes go. She's steadfast in our agreement, and I like that. Her husband Charles, also an actor, albeit not as good, well, he pretends to be my father and he seems to like kids, and together I swear they look like a fucking pharmaceutical commercial. Charles is quieter; he stays back out of the fray. He's the father I'd wished I'd had, and I have to give it to you, you nailed that one. Of course, our children, like our guests, have no idea these aren't their real grandparents, and I for one wouldn't want to ever disappoint them.

I'm thinking about what would happen if anyone knew the truth, if they would appreciate the lengths we go to, to appear normal, to fit in. I change out the overflowing trash bag, a job that's supposed to be yours, when Sharon gets my attention. Between the two of them, Anne and Sharon, you might as well be watching an Olympic sport in who can be the top bitch. It appears they are in some unspoken competition to win gold, although at times they play well together. That's not to say the game doesn't take its toll—it does. Sharon has gained thirty-five pounds in the last three months, a condition that she swears is related to her thyroid but which I contribute to being a useless cunt who drowns her sorrows in food. She pats her hair and eyes me sympathetically. "Is Jude's mother deceased?"

Deceased. Ever the cunt that she is, she even chooses useless words when what she really means is dead.

"Excuse me?" I ask and I play dumb because I'm busy, and engaging with her makes me want to stab my eyeballs out.

"Well, it's just I always see his father around, but I don't think I've ever met his mother."

I consider her question for a moment before I settle on my answer. Had I not been busy, and had I not been so pissed at you for skipping out on me, I might have chosen a different route. But in that moment, I couldn't help myself. "You know," I say, touching my chin. "That's really something you should ask Jude."

Her hand flies to her heart. "Oh, I would never," she says, as though to show she's not a monster, just an insufferable bitch.

I smile. "I figured as much," I tell her and then I excuse myself to rid myself of the trash.

She calls out, catching me off guard. "It's just that if she were— well that would explain a lot."

I turn and I tilt my head. "Like what?"

"Like how obsessed he seems to be with you."

~

LIKE HOW OBSESSED HE IS WITH YOU. THE WORDS KEEP RINGING
in my ears. They don't stop until I'm sixteen and back in that
bedroom again, happy, and sad, and full of hope to know that
there is some good in the world.

"It's not natural," my friend Carrie tells me, sipping the
rim of her coke can. We're sitting cross-legged on her bed. I
look over at the clock, and then back at her. This is my
favorite time of day, but it's also the worst, because I know
I'll have to go soon. I frown, and she reaches over, tracing the
skin on my ankle. It gives me goosebumps, and she laughs,
offering me her soda. I take it, not because I like soda— my
father swears it'll make me fat— but because I'll be tired later
in class, and it always seems to help.

"I know," I say, and I swallow. I know where this is going,
it's what she always wants to discuss—the reason we have to
meet like this. She doesn't understand why we can't see each
other outside of school. I can't let her.

"I think he's obsessed with you," she says, and she
narrows her gaze.

I shake my head. "He's just overprotective."

"Obsessed," she says, tickling me, and I don't like it when
she does this because I'm afraid we're going to wake her
parents. No doubt they'll tell my dad, and then the one good
thing, the one friend I have, will be taken away, like everything else.

"Stop," I plead, and she laughs louder. I shush her.

"It's not fair," she says, and I know. I've heard it all before.

"Life isn't fair."

"Well," she says, looking at the time. She pouts. "For the
record, he's not the only one."

I smile because it's nice to have a friend after all these years.

And then she leans in and kisses me, and everything changes.

～

I CAN'T SHAKE MY IRRITATION. I DON'T LIKE PEOPLE PUTTING their nose where it doesn't belong, and who knew having friends would be so much work? I take the trash out to the outdoor bin, and I end up walking around the side of the house to try to catch some air. Your father is standing there, staring at the grass, and instantly I wonder what would happen if Sharon had asked *him* about your mother. Maybe I should have suggested as much— if nothing else because I've never quite gotten around to it myself. It's not that I haven't wanted to, it's just that I know about picking my battles and I know about driving wedges, and well, he's been a bit better about us, since the children came along.

"Some party," he says, and I can't tell whether he means it as a good thing or not.

"Yeah," I say. "Olivia is happy."

"How would you know?" He asks, and it catches me off guard.

"Because I'm her mother."

"Maybe—" he says, and if it's meant to be a blow, it is. "But you've spent so much time trying to impress the neighbors I can't see how you'd know if you were wrong."

I wait for a moment. Giving him time to gloat. "It's really too bad..." I tell him as I stuff the trash in the can. I pause holding the lid. "That Jude's mother couldn't be here today."

He meets my eye, but he doesn't say anything in return. He doesn't have to.

~

I DON'T KNOW WHAT HAS GOTTEN INTO PEOPLE TODAY, thinking they can talk to me any way they want to, but it appears they're confused about who they're dealing with, and obviously, I'm going to have to step up my game. He's your father, and I can't fault you for wanting him here, even if I don't. If there's a silver lining to any of it, it turns me on how very assertive you become in his presence, as though you're the one who's in control here, as though, I'm not giving you a run for your money every step of the way. One thing is for sure, you don't let your father see you sweat; hell, you don't let anyone see you sweat. Not even me. But this morning in the foyer, standing over the dead babysitter, you couldn't quite help yourself, could you? It radiated off you, the weight of it all. The killing, the lying, the hiding, the pretending. I wanted to take you in my arms then, to tell you that we'll work it out, that we always do, that we are good together, you and I. I wanted to promise you I won't ever let things get stale. And now I realize that maybe Sharon's question about your mother was a gift—hand delivered—a reminder that maybe it's time to stop hiding and get to the bottom of things.

~

YOU'RE STILL NOWHERE TO BE FOUND, AND IT'S ME WHO'S sweating now. The fake grandparents have taken the children outside for the magic show, and the adults have congregated in our kitchen, and I'm mentally going through my checklist, careful not to miss a thing— hell-bent that this party will go off without a hitch. I don't care what your father says about my brown-nosing. We need these people to like us. It's unfortunate, but without their buy-in, our children stand little chance among their peers in school, and every species of animal knows it's important to stand together. No one wants their child to be the outcast. It's certain death, in the wild, and apparently, in suburbia too. It's obvious we have to dot our Is and cross our Ts, which is fairly hard to do when you skip out at birthday parties, you know.

I almost forgive your faux pas—making murder more important than cake, but then what could be more important than cake, if not murder. I can't say, and apparently neither can you, which is why I silently pray that they extend that magic show long enough for you to reappear, although currently I'm not so sure.

To make matters worse, Sharon is rattling on and on about fundraising for a new technology teacher, and God, I hate her. I pretend to listen as I silently plot her murder, even if I know I can't technically go through with it. Not here, anyway. Seriously though, these kids are five years old, what could they possibly need a technology teacher for? To derail the terrible thoughts I'm having about choking her out, I ask as much, and this is when Anne chimes in and seals the deal. She smiles sweetly and addresses the crowd, instead of me, and this is always the first clue about how something is going to go down with these women. She pats her chest—always drawing attention to money well spent— and then she clears her throat, ready to deliver her speech. "I can only assume that you aren't well read on what our children are up against in a global market, Kate," she says, looking at everyone *but* me. "I mean… I get it. I do. I know if my Stanley were away as much as your Jude seems to be, well…I'd hardly have time to read either. But I'm with Sharon on this one. This is important, and well-read or not—you have to realize that. We have to think long-term about our children's futures."

I grit my teeth but I recover quickly. *For our children's*

future. "No," I say waving her off. "I suppose you're right," I tell her as I scrub at a stain in the granite, one I know won't come off. Knowing only makes me scrub harder. Mostly, though I start thinking long-term.

∿

ONCE OUR ENTIRE KITCHEN HAS BEEN SCRUBBED CLEAN IN front of our guests, I excuse myself politely and I run upstairs to grab what I need. By the time I return, the room is seemingly divided, with the women off to one side, their men on the other. The men discuss sports, and luckily, I've made sure to memorize a few facts, and I insert them where appropriate. In making the rounds between the two groups, I transform into the perfect hostess, and as such, I make sure to slip a little something extra into Anne's drink. It's not quite the lethal dose I would prefer, just enough to do the trick, because I've done the math and I've thought long-term on this one. No one talks down to me and gets away with it forever. Certainly not twice in the span of twenty-four hours, and I guess you could say karma rhymes with Kate.

"I think you might want to cut Anne off," I eventually whisper to 'her Stanley,' nodding in her direction. I give it time, before calling attention to her. I've taken care to top off drinks yet again and I've put out another fruit tray. He looks at me as though I'm crazy, and maybe he's on to something. But he, too, will learn. "I've refilled her glass three times per her request and… you know, Jude makes his signature sangrias pretty strong…"

"Ah, Anne's no lightweight," he slurs. He raises his glass to his mouth and then pauses realizing he has something to say. "Let me tell you about our college days…" he continues boisterously, which makes it clear, he's for sure had one too many.

"Maybe some other time" I offer, slipping away. He looks disappointed and well... yuck. I offer my friendliest smile as consolation. "I need to check on the kids."

"Suit yourself," I hear him call after me, and I don't know what is worse than a middle-aged drunk man. "But I've got stories for days whenever you're ready!" He adds, and like his wife, he is relentless.

I make my way around the house in search of you and also Sarah, Anne's 'Girl Friday.' Unsurprisingly, you're still nowhere to be found, and so I send you a text. You don't reply, at least not right away, and as I roam the house staring down at my phone, I finally run in to Sarah as she's coming out of the bathroom. She's tall and thin, gaunt if you ask me, although she does have a certain look about her, as though she could have been a fashion model a decade and several vials of Botox ago. Despite the fact that she and Anne are 'besties'— their word not mine— I don't altogether hate Sarah. I feel sorry for her, actually. She's the kind of woman who would ask how high if you were to tell her to jump, the kind who would crawl out of her skin at the word boo in a well-lit room.

"Hey," I say to her, and she seems out of breath. She always seems that way, and for someone who practically lives in spin class, I'll never understand. But it isn't exactly unsexy, this breathing thing she does, and if Sarah weren't such a pushover, she's the kind of girl I could be attracted to. "Hey," she smiles, and you wouldn't believe it but she seems genuinely happy to see me. "Great party—" she adds just before I cut her off.

"Listen," I say, lowering my voice. "You might want to keep an eye on Anne. I can't help but notice...she's had several glasses of sangria and well, it's just...Jude mixes them pretty strong..."

She purses her lips. "Hmm," she says and I can tell she

wants to make the right move, to say the right thing. "I'll check on her," she tells me finally. "But you know Anne—" she adds flicking her tiny wrist. "She's always on top of things. And she isn't really a heavy drinker…"

"You're right," I reply with a slight nod. "I'm sure she's fine," I say, and I shake my head to show how ridiculous my sentiment was. "I just wanted to say something…you know —" I lower my voice and she leans in, always seeking approval, this one. "Just in case."

"I—" she starts to reply but all hell breaks loose instead.

The noise is deafening, and suddenly, it becomes clear that a car alarm is going off, and it's coming from our garage. One of the moms, I'm fairly certain her name is Susan, rushes in like she's playing hot potato, as though what she's holding is burning her hands. "James found a set of keys in the couch, and I'm so sorry—" she exclaims, her voice full of guilt as she holds them out. I don't let her finish. Instead, I take the keys from her and rush to the garage, only to find that 'Anne's Stanley' has beaten me there.

And it's worse than it seems. Not only is he in our garage, in close proximity to the dead body in your trunk, he has the driver's side door open, and he appears to be fishing around in a very bad attempt to turn off the alarm. I press the button on the keys to disable it myself, only it doesn't do the trick. I press again, holding the button down. But the alarm blares on, and it's so loud I can hardly think. But what has crossed my mind is how painful I'm going to make your death whenever you get back here. I swear Jude, this was not the time to pull a disappearing act. I let up and then I press the button again, still to no avail; the keys are sticky and the button doesn't budge. Nothing is working, except that the trunk has popped, and I'm not sure if it's me or Stanley who caused this cluster-fuck of a situation, in our vain attempts to stop the noise. But who is at fault matters little when it's actually your fault, for not being here, for not fixing this, for insisting we put the dead girl in the trunk in the first place. I lift the hood and yank the cord for the battery, which stops the noise instantly. Stanley looks amazed, as though he's never seen under the hood of a car in his life, and somehow I wouldn't doubt that. Afterward, in the blissful silence, I make my move to go and close the trunk, only unfortunately, Stanley starts to follow suit. I stop abruptly, and I reach behind me for the shovel, anything to disable him, should he get too close. As my fingers brush the handle he smiles at me, and I sort of feel bad for what I'm about to do, but sometimes people are too helpful.

"Stanley," I hear a male voice call out over the alarm. "Come quick," I hear another say. I exhale and loosen my grip on the handle. As he turns to go, I sigh, placing the shovel back in its rightful place. Then I close the trunk and I realize even though this close call was your fault— you couldn't have taken your car because you didn't have the keys. Still, that doesn't make me any less angry at you for putting me in this position.

Stanley has just about made it around to the front of your car when I hear someone say, "It's Anne. Something has happened in the bathroom." He turns to look at me ever so briefly as though I hold the answers and I do. Then he turns on his heel and rushes in and I can't help but exhale the breath I hadn't realized I'd been holding. I lean against the wall, savoring the sweet silence, and I say a silent thank you because what a pity it would have been, had something happened to the both of them.

∾

I SQUEEZE THROUGH THE CROWD THAT HAS GATHERED AROUND the downstairs bathroom, and as I make my way inward I can see that Anne is splayed out on the bathroom floor. Her husband, and another of the fathers, is knelt over her. Her sundress is up over her hips, her underwear and everything else on full display. She looks better naked than I'd imagined; I'll give her that. In fact, the scene gives me great pleasure, but I don't lose sight of the fact that there's still work to be done. "Has anyone called 9-1-1?" I call out into the crowd, and that's when I see Sarah hovered by the front door. She's speaking into a cell phone, her hand cupped over the receiver. She meets my eye and raises her free hand to let me know she's on top of it. I have no doubt that in her mind, there's guilt. She's a little too late— I warned her— but then, sometimes life gives us lemons, and sometimes we forget to make lemonade. Sarah was a bad friend; she failed to heed my warning and it's apparent in her eyes that she's secretly afraid this will get back to Anne when all is said and done. She has a right to be afraid; I can't make any promises, and animal instinct is a powerful thing, isn't it?

I make my way out to the backyard in search of the fake grandparents and of course, Rudy. He needs to see this. Luckily, everyone out back is oblivious to the madness, as are our littlest partygoers, and thankfully so. I will admit that I take pleasure in letting them know we have a situation and that you're nowhere to be found. Jane and Charles agree, along with several other parents, to keep the children outside while Rudy insists on staying on my heels. He sounds exactly like you as he rattles off questions but when the fire department arrives he finally backs off and directs them in. Eventually, with help on the scene, the crowd disperses, but only a little. Stanley leans across the frame of the bathroom door, sweat and alcohol dripping from his pores, and I can tell he is equal parts terrified and embarrassed that poor ol' Anne still hasn't come to. Maybe she was right in her initial assessment. Maybe it is poor taste to serve alcohol at a children's party.

But I didn't see her saying no, did you? Of course, you didn't, because you weren't here and in any case obviously, the drugs helped her along. However, you should know that I was generous—probably more so than I should have been, in not giving her enough to kill her. Not this time. This time, I thought of the children. I wouldn't want to ruin the party.

But then you can't know this, yet, and the medics are still working on her when you come waltzing through the door at last, holding a dozen balloons, your expression fixed. You glare at me, waiting for me to say something, and so I do. "Anne had a little too much to drink," I whisper in your ear, loud enough for others to hear. "But I'm sure she'll be fine."

You crane your neck to see and then you take my hand in yours, and you squeeze hard. So hard it hurts. You're on to me, and this is your way of saying what you mean to say without really saying anything at all.

~

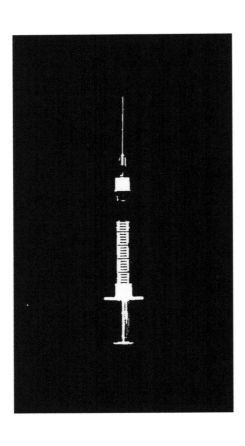

CHAPTER EIGHT

JUDE

Look what you've done now. This is bad, Kate. Last night you drugged me, but you couldn't just stop there could you? Nope. You had to go and drug our neighbor, and why can't you just hold normal grudges like other wives? Do you know how easy life could be if you were content to shop and decorate and post random garbage on social media showcasing how great your life is, instead of thriving on stirring up trouble in the form of retaliation?

I don't know what to tell you to do to fill your time. But I do know we can't go on like this. Take up a hobby—knitting or reading—anything, but preferably something that's safe for others. Maybe start a blog. Maybe that's the trick. All I know is that's what all of the other women seem to be doing these days. So, you know, maybe do that. Personally, I don't get why they think anyone other than pedophiles and their passive aggressive mommy friends give a shit about little Johnny and his every move. But I digress. This is about you.

As for me, I've just murdered a man for money. He wasn't exactly salt of the earth, but still. I'm tired. Murder is hard work. So to say it isn't comforting to come home with proverbial blood on my hands and find my living room full of law enforcement and rubber-necker neighbors is an understatement. What am I supposed to do with that? How much lower can it get? I don't know. But I do know you're getting crazier by the minute, and they warned me this happens with women.

I wanted to give you the benefit of the doubt—I still do. But you beat a dead man last night, which doesn't exactly help your case. Only that wasn't enough for you. I know because our dead babysitter is in the back of my car, and somehow you think it's okay to up the ante with an unconscious drunk woman on the bathroom floor.

AFTER THE PARTY IS OVER, AND THE PARAMEDICS HAVE TAKEN Anne away to pump her full of charcoal and shame, you send the kids home with Josie. After all that's happened, it only makes sense that you'd need a rest. Or so you say—and so she thinks.

Only instead, you and I are not resting; we have a job to do, and so we head down to the water's edge to dispose of the nanny. All in a day's work, you joke. You seem to have missed that I'm not in a joking mood.

"I don't know," you tell me as I glare out the window, surveying our surroundings. I put the car in park, and I don't really care what you do or don't know, but that's never stopped you before and it doesn't stop you now. You inhale and let it out slowly, smooth and dramatic, just to drive home your point. "I think maybe we should've taken her out to the barn."

I don't answer, and you take that as a sign you are winning. You aren't. You tighten your ponytail; it's your tell, you're ready to go to war. "It's just that dead bodies in water always seem to have a way of washing up..."

"Not if you do it right," I say, taking off my seatbelt. I turn toward you and I wait for more. You're not the only one who's ready for a fight. All the way here, you've bitched and moaned about those women, about my father, and about how tired you are, and quite frankly I'm over it.

"Whatever," you huff, and then you check yourself in the mirror as though getting rid of a body is something one needs to be presentable for. Paradoxically, it's in moments like these I find you most beautiful. Looking at you now, your profile lit by the soft glow of light coming off the mirror, my anger subsides a little. I don't understand the extremes I feel toward you, I only know I can't help myself. I start to tell you as much, but true to your nature, you don't give me the chance. "I'm just happy to get away from the kids for a little while," you exclaim, and then you proceed to drone on. It's meaningless chit-chat which I refuse to partake in and eventually, annoyed by my silence, you shift in your seat and you mirror me. "Also," you add, lowering your voice. "There's something I need to talk to you about..."

I meet your gaze, and my expression isn't exactly what you'd call friendly. I don't get why you can't just say what you need to say— but if I were a betting man, I'd wager it's because you have a vagina.

You look away again, and I see it for what it is. A sign of guilt. I watch as you chew on your bottom lip, and as much as your hesitation irritates me, there's something about it that turns me on too. You're teasing me, seeing how far you can get, and it works, you have my attention. Finally, you decide to quit messing around. "It's about Brady."

"What about him?" I ask impatiently. I hadn't expected it to be this.

You shift in your seat, and you stare straight ahead, out

the windshield, at something far off. It's dark, and I know you're unsure and so you don't answer, at least not right away.

It isn't like you to start something without finishing it, and this forces me to press for more. "Kate?"

You exhale and then you trace your eyelids with the tips of your fingers. "You know what…" you start and then you pause and shift. "Never mind," you add, and I watch as you sit up a little straighter. You mess with your hair, and you aren't focused. "I'm sure it's nothing."

"Kate." I urge, and you look over at me because my tone comes out harsh. It was meant to.

"I'm just worried about Monique's fall…"

"You mean you're worried about Brady?"

"Yes."

I rub my jaw. "You mean, you're worried about how much he saw?" I ask, because I read you well, and you're better at being a mother than you think.

You tilt your head slightly and you study my face. "Yeah."

I place my hand on yours. "Kids are resilient," I tell you. You look away for a second, and then over at me again. Your expression is blank but eventually you smile.

MY LEAST FAVORITE PART OF ANY GIG IS DISPOSING OF THE body, if the job calls for it. It's the worst part, mostly because it's what tends to get people caught. Also, it's messy and not at all simple. Even worse is disposing of a body you hadn't planned to have to dispose of. So to say I'm irritated at having to do this would be putting it mildly. Also, I can tell you think you're going to get away with letting me do the dirty work here—but that's where you're wrong. You're still wearing the dress you wore to the party—with sandals—, and I have absolutely no idea why you couldn't have come more prepared. I'm not sure how you plan on submerging a body wearing *that*, but then, I guess that's your problem, not mine. You don't realize it yet, but I'm onto you. You're trying to get out of work by pissing me off, by worrying me, by wearing the wrong thing. But it won't work. Not this time.

Determined to get this over and done, I turn off the ignition, press the button to pop the trunk, and look over at you. You look weary but you're the reason we're here to begin with—if it weren't for you, we wouldn't have a dead girl in the back of my car. We'd be at home, putting our children to bed, where we belong. I start to tell you this, because it's been a long day, and it needs to be said, but you catch me off guard when you open the door and climb out without saying anything, without the push-back I expected. I watch in the rearview mirror as you walk around to the back of the car. You close the trunk. You're dead set on going to the barn, you've said so a million times. But I've already made my decision, and so I remove the keys from the ignition and follow your lead. There's still a part of me that hopes you'll surprise me, that maybe you're willing to get your hands dirty. Sooner rather than later would be better, because it's nearly pitch black out, save for the headlights, and we haven't got time to dilly dally out in the woods. It's eerie out here, even for me.

"What are you doing?" I ask, watching as you hoist yourself up onto the top of the trunk.

You reach for me in the glow of the brake lights, and you pull me in close. I let you, and I know this is a bad idea.

"I need to feel something," you say, and then I feel something, and that something is your teeth grazing my neck. You know what gets me, and I hate you just a little for that.

You spread your legs wider, and it's convenient you don't wear panties. "Jude," you say, and I know what comes next by the way you say my name and it's *you*. "I want you to fuck me," you plead, and well, you know me. I've always been a sucker for good manners and a woman who knows what she wants.

∼

YOU'RE DIGGING YOUR NAILS INTO MY BACK WHEN I HEAR THE words echo through my ears and settle in my solar plexus. My throat constricts and then suddenly, my world goes still.

"Freeze! Hands up! Police," the deep voice calls out once again, as though it hadn't done the trick the first time.

Your breath catches as I take my hands off of you. I hold them in the air and you look into my eyes and you're searching for something. I'm not sure what that something is, reassurance perhaps, but there's something else in your expression, too. Anger, I think, maybe a little bit of mischief, and I swear Kate, now is not the time for that.

"Turn around slowly," the officer instructs, and what else could I possibly do with my pants undone and my dick hanging out?

Not much, apparently, and so I do as he says. He flickers his flashlight from me to you, the light is blinding. I hear your breath quicken, and it makes me uneasy. You know there's a gun in my right pocket, and I say a silent prayer that you don't do anything drastic.

"Move," the officer orders and I scoot out from between your knees and move to the side just a little in order to allow you some decency, but also so you can't reach the gun. Only, you don't immediately move to close your legs, and this pisses me off more than you know.

"Well, well, well... look what we have here," he says, blinding me with his flashlight once again. "I would've guessed you was two teenagers, out here doin' the dirty—

but nope. Look at you. You're old enough to know better..."

"Can we help you, officer?" You ask in the worst southern accent I've ever heard, and this is when I realize how fucked we are. Who says shit like that at a time like this? He's just caught us screwing in the woods, on private property—of course, we can't help him. We've offered him a handful of charges, wrapped neatly with a fucking bow, and handed it to him on a silver platter. I'd say we've already helped him enough. I sigh, and I can't believe you're going to play it this way, but obviously you are, and I can be a lot of things, Kate —but a cop killer isn't one of them. So it would really do us both some good if you'd take my long, heavy sigh for what it is—a sign that you'd better not fuck this up.

He laughs at your stupidity, and immediately I can hear there's something off in the sound of it. "Yeah, actually you can, darlin," he tells you, stepping forward, too close for my comfort. "I was just lookin' for a good time, and here I came upon you two gettin' it on in the woods. Can't say we get that kind of excitement out here in these parts very often..."

Somehow I doubt that, I think. But apparently you don't know how to think thoughts without speaking them. "I'd guess not," you say to him, and I shake my head. I can't believe I let you get me into this. We should have just disposed of the body like we planned— but no—you had to go and distract me, and now here we are instead in hillbilly hell with a cop that seems straight out of a B-rated movie.

"You kids got ID?"

"Of course, officer," you say in the worst sultry voice I've ever heard. But your act doesn't stop there. It gets a lot worse before it gets better. You exhale slowly, too slowly, and you scoot forward just a tad, drawing your dress further up on your hips, and it's no accident, you know exactly what you're doing. And I swear to God if you show that redneck bastard any more of what's mine you're about to be the second female I know to die today.

"It's in the car," I say, interrupting your peep show, and he points his weapon at my face. Fuck. He's a jumpy one, and that can't be good. Also, it's clear, he likes talking to you better.

"Who asked you?" he says, and I take it as confirmation. He steps forward again, and fuck, it's obvious where this is going. I've seen enough of those homemade videos to know how this scenario goes down. This bastard hasn't seen much in the way of action— but he wants to—and now I'm going to have to kill this motherfucker in order to save myself, and this is all your fault.

"Sir. SIR," you call out in what appears to be a lame attempt to diffuse the situation. You realize too that one shot is all it would take, and we're out in the middle of fucking nowhere, with a shitty cop who has a vendetta, and we aren't exactly innocent are we?

He turns his attention to you, and I have to give you credit. Maybe your plan isn't so lame after all. "Why don't you be a lady and grab it for me, hon'," he orders, motioning in your direction. Still, he steadies his gun on me. "You, cowboy," he says his voice drawn low. "I want you to turn around slowly and place your hands on the car."

I do as he says, and this is when I know for sure. I'm going to have to take him out, and it's going to have to happen soon.

"You know what an indecency charge'll do to ya these days, boy?" he asks, and I don't— but that's okay—I'll make damned sure it never comes to that.

"It'll get you on one of those kiddie watch lists," he tells me, and that's when I decide I've officially had enough.

"Fuck you," I tell him and I rear backward, ready to end this. I head butt him, although he's quick, and all of a sudden he's aiming pepper spray directly at my face. It feels like there are a thousand fire ants stinging my eyeballs and I can't breathe. But that's not enough for him, because in the next second it escalates, and before I know it, I'm on the ground involuntarily rolling in the dirt. He's tasing me, and I have no fucking idea where you are, because my whole world has gone dark. All I know now, is I don't give a fuck if you show him you're crazy, because he deserves it and this sick bastard, he'll get what's coming to him, one way or another. I can promise you that.

"Here it is," I hear you call from somewhere that feels very far off. Your voice seems desperate, and I'd hoped you would do better than that. He places cuffs around my wrists, and if I'd thought this situation couldn't possibly get any worse, I was wrong.

Buying time, but mostly because I'm half out of it and drooling, I let him cuff me without a fight. As he attempts to haul me up, however, I weigh my options and I conclude, fuck it; I'll take the bullet.

I hear you pleading as he pulls me up to a standing position. I stumble forward a little, and he orders you to stay put and then he kicks my feet out from under me. He's showing off for you, and you're making this worse. He laughs as he pushes my head down onto the trunk. Hard. He holds it there, in the palm of his hand, and even though my ears are ringing, I swear I'll never forget that laugh so long as I live. As I consider all the ways I plan to extinguish this motherfucker, I can hear that you're speaking to him in a hushed tone. I can't make out exactly what is being said, I only hear the static of his radio come in and out. Using my left foot I do my best to inch my pants up my leg just a little. If I can just reach my gun, I can get out of this the easy way. *And this is exhibit A of why you never let them take the first shot, I hear my father say.* All of my training, all of the tactics I've learned over the years, everything that's been drilled in comes down to this very moment—whether or not I can get out of the bind you've gotten me in. Never trust a woman, my father always said, and maybe there's something to that.

"It's your lucky day," he tells me as he leads me up to a standing position once again, only this time he hauls me up by my hair. I start to kick backward, but there's the issue with my pants, and in turn my attempt does nothing. I try to find you in the dark but I can't see anything given the pepper spray and the blood that's trickling down my forehead and into my eyes. And for reasons I can't name, I go against everything I know, which is idiotic, seeing that this is what got me into this mess. Still, I've seen you work magic, and I decide to give you the benefit of the doubt and this is why I walk with him when he instructs me to.

"Hang tight in here," he orders, and he laughs as he does his best to force me down into the back of his squad car. But I know better than to let him put me in that car. And I'm certainly not going to hang tight and leave you out here alone with this dirty pig, which is why I make the move I do, only to be thwarted once again. This time it's his baton that puts me in my place. The blow knocks the wind out of me, and I'm being tased again, and I can't help but think if I hadn't gotten caught with my pants around my ankles this might all have turned out differently.

∾

CHAPTER NINE

KATE

I drive extra careful on the way home checking the rearview mirror approximately every 2.5 seconds. Bile rises in my throat and I want to pull over to throw up but I can't let you know the extent of the damage that asshole has done. Equally, I can't be sure he won't be there on the side of the road waiting. I wouldn't put it past that sick bastard to follow us home. But then why would he? He already has our information. You don't know this, of course. You think I gave him the fake ID's and I meant to, I really did. Until I couldn't find yours, and well, I was so worried about you taking the beating, that I did what I had to do in the moment.

"Did he hurt you?" you ask once again. You slur your words as you speak, and your gaze is off. Understandably. Still, it's starting to worry me the way you keep asking the same question over and over. He tased you twice, which explains some of your anger. Also, I'm pretty sure you have a concussion. But then maybe this is just you, you're always this intense, so it's hard to tell. I get it. You want to know if he hurt me—if I'm all right— and I am, and no, he didn't.

"What did he do to you?" you demand, and you have a

head wound, which is bleeding profusely, but you just sit and stare at me. I think you want a fight. But you're clearly not in fighting shape.

"Nothing," I tell you and I don't know why you have to be so stubborn. What happened is nothing you need to know— not right now— not like this. But it isn't like you to lose, and so you're angry and your ego is wounded— but that's life, Jude. Sometimes you win, and sometimes you lose, and it happens to everyone at one point or another. All I can do is chalk it up to the fact that you were tired, given what has transpired over the past twenty-four hours.

And the truth is, I'm not exactly lying. He didn't hurt me, not really. Surely, though you can hear it in my voice. You know I'm not telling you the whole truth, and I can only assume this is why you go for the jugular.

"Please tell me he didn't rape you, Kate," you say, which is blunt enough in and of itself, not to mention a bit uncaring, and yet it's what you add after that pisses me off most. "Because if he did, we need to see a doctor."

The 'we' part of your statement gets me, and so I reach over and backhand you, and I would feel bad given your less than stellar state, but I don't because that was an asshole thing to say. For one, you posed it as a statement, not a question, and the condescending nature of your tone is clear. You're blaming me for this— as though it's somehow my fault. Even so, slapping you doesn't make me feel any better. So I try the truth on for size.

"No," I tell you. "Of course, he didn't."

You breathe a sigh of relief, a loud one, and I let you have your moment.

"He didn't have to," I say watching your face. "I gave him what he asked for…"

You look over at me and I can see that you're afraid of what that might be. You take a deep breath and you hold it.

You're hesitant to ask and you should be. At the same time, you realize you can't not know and so you let the words roll off your tongue in spite of your fear. "And what was that?"

I press my lips together. "A lap dance."

I watch as you stir in your seat, and then you pinch the bridge of your nose. "I'm going to kill that motherfucker."

"You're lucky he didn't ask for a blow job, or I would've handled the matter for you," I retort. You aren't amused.

Instead, you turn your attention elsewhere, focusing out the passenger window and you refuse to say anything more.

"I'm sorry," I say even though we both know I don't mean it.

You take a long pull off the thick air that hangs between us and then you let it out. I watch as it fogs up the window.

"Tomorrow," you say, and then you pause and you look over at me. "I plan to head out early. Before you're up. I need to handle the issue in the trunk. ALONE this time."

"Fine," I tell you, and I smile, even though nothing that was said is anything worth smiling over. But I know how much you love that word, and I enjoy rubbing salt in your wound.

"Hey Jude," I say after several moments pass. You look over at me.

"Remember, when I said we should have gone out to the barn instead?"

You look away. But I don't stop there. I've already taken aim. This time I pull the trigger. "Can we just agree I was right?"

≈

AFTER WE GET HOME AND YOU GET WASHED UP, JOSIE CALLS and tells me Olivia has been crying and wants to come home, and that for the past two hours Brady has been sitting in the corner staring at the wall. Given the events of this shitty day, I ask Josie if she'll bribe Olivia to stay, and thankfully she says she will. As for Brady, well, she knows he does that sometimes. He is your son, after all. Early on, back when we first noticed there was something off about his behavior, something off in the way he never sleeps, in how he obsesses over things, you asked the pediatrician about it. I'm sure you remember because I didn't speak to you for three weeks afterward. They wanted us to run tests, and you insisted even though I told you it was unnecessary; I told you it didn't matter what they found. It was already clear: he has trouble dealing with emotions, and what did you expect?

It mattered little to you that his IQ was off the charts, only that he was different, and something shifted in you then, although I'm not sure what, because well, apparently I'm bad with emotions, too.

The phone rings again, causing me to jump. It's Josie again.

"Kate," she says, and her voice is panicked. "Um…I don't know how to say it so I'll just spit it out— I think there's something you should know…"

"Okay," I reply, treading carefully.

I listen as she takes a deep breath and it isn't like Josie to overreact. Eventually, she exhales. It's painfully long and I don't like the sound of it. "Olivia is crying about Monique."

"Monique?" I somehow manage to say around the lump that's formed in my throat.

"Yeah," she tells me her voice barely audible. I hear kids in the background and then I hear a door close. There's shuffling, and finally, she speaks. "She says she's scared Monique will come back."

"Why would she be scared of Monique?" I ask.

"Because she said she has been locking Brady in the

closet. Whenever you're not home. She says it's his 'punishment time.'"

My lungs empty, and I can't breathe. Words fail me for a few seconds, but afraid of what else she might say, I recover quickly. "I'm coming to get them," I say and I go.

～

IT'S THE DEAD OF NIGHT WHEN I'M FORCED STRAIGHT UP IN bed by a shrill scream. I'm surrounded by silence, and yet it reverberates off the walls. I recall the sound so clearly that I know it wasn't just in my dreams. It was real. I swear it was. Gripping the duvet, I inhale, counting to ten, and then I carefully let the breath go. Afterward, I begin my usual routine, employing all the techniques I've been told to try whenever the nightmares come. I squeeze my eyes shut, and then I open them, willing myself to adjust to the darkness.

But it's rather apparent that the techniques aren't working, because my breath is caught somewhere between my chest and my throat, and it feels like the walls are closing in. I sit up further and survey my surroundings and eventually, my eyes adjust, which helps. But only a little.

I take into account where I am, and I do my best to slow my thoughts, but I can't concentrate on anything specific, and more importantly I can't seem to suck in enough air. I count and I inhale. Over and over. Until I'm dizzy. You once told me this method was called grounding, so I'm going with that because I don't know what else to do to make the spinning stop. All I know is that being grounded sounds good. My mind races—it feels like I'm floating. I picture myself lost in space, and I'm spinning off into the void. Nothing is holding me back; nothing is tethering me to earth. I grip the sheets, squeezing harder this time, until my fingernails burn.

I'm hanging on by a thread, I realize, and my grip is slipping. I know that if I let go, there's no turning back.

I urge myself to think, to try and recall the nightmare. But when I do it only gets worse. I squeeze my eyes shut, and I see that cop with his disgusting breath and his hands on my chest, and I can feel my stomach turn. I'm going to throw up. I feel it coming any second now, and I remember how much you hate throw up. Relying on the moonlight that filters through the balcony's glass doors, I reach over and fumble around the nightstand in search of my cell phone. I'm not getting out of this bed without light to take me where I need to go. Thankfully the phone lights up when my fingers graze the screen. I pause for a second, looking over at you, sleeping next to me, quiet, content and I'm almost envious. Part of me wants to wake you. I want to ask for your help, and I almost do, but you're still angry with me when all I did was save your ass. In turn, I'm angry at you for being angry at me, and we're stuck in some sort of holding pattern, the two of us, playing this beautiful blame game in which no one wants to concede.

But I don't have time for envy or anger or much else, because my heart is pounding and it's all I can do to keep the nausea at bay. I can't make myself get up, but I can't make myself stay here either. The sound of my pulse whooshes loudly, reverberating in my ears. My feet are on standby, and my eyes are peeled—all senses are on alert.

It occurs to me to pick up the video monitors to check on the kids, although I know they are fine. They, like their father, are sleeping soundly. But not me, I am floating off. I'm lightheaded, and I can't seem to stop whatever it is that's coming. When I'm afraid I'm going to pass out, I shake you.

"Jude," I say, pressing the button on my phone so that it lights up again. I need to see light. I need you.

You open your eyes, but just barely, and you raise your brow sleepily. But you don't speak.

"I heard something."

Hearing the panic in my voice, you sit up and you listen for a moment. You ask if I've checked the monitors, and I give you a look only married people understand. You sit there for a few moments, waiting. I watch as your expression changes slowly, as indifference passes over your features and settles in. I realize we're going nowhere when you pat my leg and ask if I've had 'one of those dreams again.' It's a gesture I understand all too well. It's your way of telling me you think I'm crazy without actually saying it.

"No," I whisper. "I really heard something. And I'm pretty sure it was a scream."

"Hmm," you say, and you pause, and right when I think you're going to be useful you say what is quite possibly the dumbest thing yet. "Well, let me know if you hear it again."

As I study your face, I wonder how we wound up here, how out of all the people on this planet, I ended up with you.

You don't wait for a response. You simply yawn and settle back in.

"What if he shows up here?"

"Who?" you ask even though I'm pretty sure you know exactly who.

"The cop?"

"He won't."

"But you don't know that. What if he knows where we live?"

"I hope he does. It'll save me the trouble of going looking for him." You close your eyes and then open them again. "Which I intend to do tomorrow—so, if you don't mind...I could really use some sleep."

I'm shocked by your answer and I briefly consider admitting that I gave him our address. But I know better because I know your answer isn't a serious one, I know you just want to go back to sleep and so you'll tell me what I want to hear, which is exactly what you do.

"What if it was him who left that note in the hotel?"

"The cop?" You ask again and I've never known you to be this dense.

"Yes. The fucking cop."

"I'd say that's a long shot."

"But not impossible."

You turn over. "If he'd known we'd murdered a man, I can guarantee we wouldn't be here in this bed right now—arguing about it. Losing sleep."

I roll my eyes even though I'm aware that you can't see it in the dark with your back turned. I hope you felt it. You didn't. I can tell by the way you sleepily offer your best Band-Aid, when you suggest for the umpteenth time that we move.

"Run and you'll always be running," I tell you. It's a platitude, meant to shut you up, a slight jab between married people, a sentiment that puts old arguments to bed. I don't mean it. I'm simply reminding you of what you once told me. I'm driving the point home.

You let out a long sigh, and I expect that you'll provide some additional useless wisdom, only you proceed to righteously fall back to sleep. In a matter of minutes you're snoring again. It's a light snore, somewhere between the full-on, no-holds-barred sound you make when you're really tired, and that throaty thing you do that lets me know you're on your way there.

I know you're tired. I am too. But it irritates me that you don't take me seriously, about the screams and about other things. And, just as I'm ready to wake you again, to tell you as much, I hear it again. A scream so unmistakable, there's no denying that's what it is. It's all panic and afterward there's just silence. Nothingness.

I listen closely, waiting for more, and I tiptoe toward the window. Roscoe is waiting there, already, staring out, and I lean down and pat his head. His tongue hangs out, he's panting and his breathing picks up pace. "You heard it too," I say into the darkness, into the blank space of the early hours and he's smarter than you. I know because he begins circling. He senses it. Something is wrong. Someone is out there and my mind can't help but go to the dead body in the trunk—or to the cop in the woods, his hands roaming my body. It was bad out there. Worse than I told you. I know I'll get over it eventually, particularly once he's dead. But for now, the cut is fresh and deep. It stings. And even though it isn't the first bad thing to happen to me, the first bully to put his hands on me, I can't seem to shake this feeling. He violated me out there. It wasn't rape, but it's hard to draw lines when you're forced to do something you don't want to do. It's hard to say no when you're backed into a corner. All the while, he touched me, I thought about the kids and I kept my cool. Let him do this, I told myself over and over. Give him what he wants, or you'll lose the only thing that really matters, your children. It helped some— at least it took my mind off what he was doing, but I'm not sure it was enough. Now I know, here in the darkness, without a doubt, that I should've killed him when I had the chance. What he did will haunt me until I get revenge. It haunted me at the time, but killing a cop is not only difficult to get away with, it's no joke in the legal system, and right now I'd like to ask you where would that leave them. I want to ask you what happens if he shows up here. What happens if I can't get these thoughts out of my mind? Only, you're asleep, and there are things I can't tell you because I know if I do, you'll kill him yourself, and as angry as I am—I'm not sure I have it in me to force your hand. Anger does things to a person, and you aren't someone who kills out of anger, not like me. If one isn't careful, anger can get the best of you. It'll trip you up, trick you into getting yourself caught.

I consider this as I lean closer to the glass door, trying to get a better look, but not so close as to be seen. As I peer out, I do my best to gauge which direction the sound came from, but our street is pitch black, and I see nothing. There isn't a single light on, zero movement, nothing. All I hear are cicadas and the dog's breathing, and it feels like Roscoe and I are the only ones in the world up at this hour— but it's obvious we aren't. I know because there was the scream. I wait by the door, shifting from foot to foot.

Then I wait some more. I almost give up. In fact, I'm just about to go back to bed when four houses down, at the Morris's house, I see the faint glow of reverse lights. I watch as the car backs out of the drive. It turns in my direction, and the first thing I notice is that its headlights aren't on. As it gets closer, I can see that it's an older model— a dark blue, maybe black, station wagon. I can't remember if I've ever seen this car at their place before. I wait for the car to pass, and as it does I strain to see the plates. It's too dark to see much, and with its headlights off, it makes it impossible. Frustrated, I go to my notebook, the one I keep beside my bed so I can note the number of night wakings our son has, and I jot this down: Single driver, male. Shoulders definitely too broad to be female. Couldn't make anything else out. Strained to see plates as he passed. It could have been Anne's husband Stanley, but then it could have been anyone. He didn't seem to be in a hurry as he drove away. But then, neither would I.

~

SOMETIME JUST AFTER DAWN YOU WAKE ME WHEN YOU PLACE A cup of coffee on the bedside table. It's your version of a peace offering and at this point, I'm exhausted enough that it might just work. I squint my eyes, peeking out, unwilling and unable to open them fully. I see that you're heading to the shower and it's no different than any other morning except that it is. I watch you as you stop, and leaning halfway out the bathroom door you beckon me to join. I half want to but I can't force myself to get up. According to my notes, Brady was up three more times *after* I heard the screams, and twice before. It doesn't escape me that I only know these details because I've written them down, a fact I find sad. Or rather, at least *I think* there were screams. By the light of day, it's all fuzzy, the hours and the sleeplessness, it blurs together and I can't say I'm sure of anything. All I know is that I have a vague recollection of dread. This leads me to grab my notebook and study my chicken scratch. After the notes about the night wakings, of which the doctors swear there is no explanation, I wrote: Something has happened.

Studying the words on the page, I do my best to try to remember why there's a pit in the bottom of my stomach, aside from the fact that our four year old won't sleep, and it takes several seconds to jar my memory. I vaguely recall seeing reverse lights. My mind flashes to a dead guy in a hotel room, to the nanny at the bottom of the stairs, to you in the woods on the ground, to the unconscious woman on our bathroom floor, and then to another man's hands up my dress. Carefully, I piece it all together, like a jigsaw, the circumstances of each event. It's overwhelming. But eventually they fit together. My stomach churns, and I lean over and vomit into the wastebasket that you keep on your side of the bed. When I recover, I pick up the notebook again. I study the ink as it bleeds under my thumb. I've rubbed it into the page, smeared it in but the words remain nonetheless. *Something has happened.*

When I read back over the rest of my notes, my heart

sinks. Maybe it wasn't a scream, maybe the voices are coming back, and you've warned me about getting up so many times in the night. You tell me Brady doesn't need me, you want me to let him be, but how can I just let him cry? You don't know, that's what you always say. You tell me you read that a lack of sleep only contributes to mental disorders, and of course you can't be bothered, because you have important work to do. You can't— and you won't— be kept up at all hours by a child who refuses to sleep.

Even so—of all things, you might be right about, I hope it's not this one. The voices. It's been years, I've lived for years without them—so long I thought I was in the clear. But if I'm honest, there is a part of me who knew this wouldn't— that it *couldn't* last forever. Sitting here now, my tongue coated in vomit, my stomach churning, I feel it. You're right. They're looming, rising up, waiting for the chance to pounce. So much has happened in the last few days. All of it, so fast. Too many things have been left undone—too much is beyond my control. And it's always in times like these they show themselves—in times I'm unsure. They're smart and they wait, clawing their way back in slowly until they catch me off guard, seeping into every corner of my consciousness.

This can't be happening. Not again and not now. I look over at the dog as I consider my next move. He's still at the window. "Something is up," I whisper. He peers back at me, briefly, before turning his attention toward the window again. He knows too. Something bad *has* happened.

The scream replays in my mind. I've heard that kind of scream before, and I know it by heart. Terror—fear— those are sounds you don't forget. A woman, maybe even a neighbor of ours, was in trouble, and I did nothing. I don't like trouble this close to home. Not when I'm out of the loop. Something ended last night, clearly. But I have a feeling it was the start of something, too.

DEAD IN THE WATER

CHAPTER TEN

JUDE

I woke up with a concussion, a head wound, and wife who isn't herself. Par for the course, these days it seems, and just a few things that kept me from getting the dead girl in the back of my trunk situation handled before dawn the way I'd planned. Also, we're fighting again, and I'm pretty sure you're losing your mind.

Plus, I know you aren't being completely honest about what that cop did to you. I know by the way you flinched as I ran my hand up your thigh, and I swear to God, Kate, just as soon as I dispose of the dead girl in my trunk, I will deal with that motherfucker in a way that will make him wish he'd never seen the likes of me—or laid a finger on you.

I guess it makes sense that after what happened last night, you would be off your game a little. But that doesn't explain the fact that you're telling me and anyone who will listen that you heard screams last night. By noon you'd already called no fewer than a handful of our neighbors. I know because I checked your phone remotely, and although they won't say it — I'm pretty sure they think you're crazy, too.

This paranoid version of you is new, and we have a

rotting corpse in our trunk and screams in the night should be the least of your worries right now. I don't get it—usually, you let me do the worrying, and I'll tell you one thing, I'm not the least bit concerned with these screams you heard, real or not. What I am concerned about is the note I had to pry from a dead guy's mouth, the impending burial I need to attend to, and the motherfucking cop I am going to have to kill. You tell me to get over it, you promise me that you're fine. But I have eyes, and I see you. You want me to let it all go—but I can't—and I won't. Cop or not, he's the one who has to go. Protect and serve—it's a motto he's bound by, and he did neither. I know because there's a dead girl in my trunk who is decomposing by the minute, and he didn't protect or serve her. He only served himself and his sick fantasies. It's not the first time he's pulled this, I can assure you of that. And you know what happens when people think they have that much power? Men who think they can force women to do what they want? They die. Maybe not right away. But eventually. There's a little saying you might know: What goes around comes around. And in this pig's case, the *what* in that sentiment is going to be me.

~

I've always been of the opinion that if you haven't got something important to say, you might as well not say anything at all. After all, *it's better to keep your mouth shut and appear stupid, than open it and remove all doubt.*

Well, speaking of mouths and keeping them shut, I can't stop thinking about that note. *'I've got my eye on you,'* who writes shit like that? It sounds like some kind of third grade fucking Valentine, if you ask me.

You say you didn't write it, that it wasn't there when you went back in, and if you're telling the truth, well—we both know what that means. Someone else was. What I want to know was *who* and *why*, and how close did we come to getting set up? Do you have any idea what would have happened, had I not gone back in and discovered that note? We'd be wanted for murder—that's what. But that's not what gets me. It's the fact that if it isn't you who wrote it, then there's someone else messing with me, and tell me Kate, if a man can't even trust his wife, then who can he trust?

I'll give you a hint. The answer is no one.

~

IT'S A CLOUDY DAY AND MUGGY, THE KIND OF DAY THAT HAS A hint of irritation in the air that you just can't shake. You say it's a full moon, and that's why all of this is happening. You actually believe in that crap, and I don't pretend that I know all the secrets of the universe, but what I do know is this: No one gets off that easy. None of this shit just happens to us, Kate. We make it happen.

Speaking of making things happen, I take the girl back to the water. There's a part of me who hopes that bastard cop shows up, but he doesn't, which is probably a good thing because I have to rush as it is. You demanded that I take her out to the barn. But I'm short on time, and digging a grave wasn't exactly a calendar item this week, and well, we have other more pressing issues going on than what constitutes a proper burial. Two new jobs came in over the course of my handling your dirty work, and you see, I can make things happen. I can make them happen, and I can make them go away. Business is booming and I live for this. In fact, I'm going to have to leave town tomorrow, and well, I know how much you hate that. I could have said no, but duty calls. Bad guys don't give up just because you're having an off day. Criminals don't stop, they don't wait for you to be ready.

Also, there's a full moon, and I think some distance will do us good.

~

I COME HOME SWEATY AND DIRTY, BUT ACTUALLY HAPPY TO SEE you, despite the sense of ever looming dread I feel over having to tell you I have to hop on a plane. Despite what you're going to say—I'm not completely oblivious. It's not that I don't realize what an inopportune time this is—given everything that's happened— is just that work is work, and you need to get ahold of yourself, and I'm coming to realize you can't very well do that if I keep handling everything for you. You know the saying: *Give a man a fish, and you feed him for a day. Teach a man to fish, and you feed him for a lifetime.*

Burying the nanny was giving you a fish. When really, what you need is to learn to fend for yourself. And I guess you could say that both my patience and my generosity has run out of line.

I'm at the end of my rope, and I don't know what I expect to find when I walk in the door, I never do, and today is no different. Except that you're laid out on the couch, and you and the kids are glued to those goddamned devices, that you insist they need. Once upon a time, they used to rush to the door the second they heard my key hit the lock. They'd tackle my knees and scream Daddy, and next to coming home to you, it was always the best part of my day. These days, though, I'm lucky if they even glance up from those screens, and now you're in on it too, and something has to change.

"Look, Daddy!" Olivia shrieks as I lean down to kiss you. "Mommy is letting us look at Jake and Izzy on Facebook."

I pull back and *really* look at you, and you smile because you know how much I hate Facebook. You're still wearing the workout clothes you had on this morning when I left, only I know for a fact you haven't worked out. Your hair's a mess, your eyes are wild—this isn't *you*, and what the fuck have I just come home to?

"I spoke with Josie..." you say, and you glare up at me. "And she heard the scream, too."

"Of course she did. Josie will tell you what you want to hear because that's Josie."

You don't reply, and Brady demands my attention.

"Look! Miss Anne is fairy..." he tells me, pointing at the screen, and I'll be damned if he's not lying. You read my expression, and you understand the question, and what the hell are you showing my children Kate? If you tell me not to worry, it's make believe, I'll tell you, you're not kidding. Because if you would've told me ten years ago that grown people would be posting pictures of themselves on the internet using filters to look like fairies and strange animals, I would've told you, you were fucking insane. Which you are. But then—it appears that this whole world is losing its goddamned mind. In fact, there's so much I want to say to you in this moment, but we have kids, and when you have kids you can't go around starting fights the way you used to. But if I could start World War III, here and now, I'd begin by letting you know that I've searched your phone and I can't believe half of the crap you look at. You say you have no time —but that's just a cover for how much you waste. Because if you want to know where all of your precious time goes, I'll tell you. About two to three hours of it goes toward scrolling through this bullshit. And that's just what I've accounted for.

You swear we need a nanny because you're overwhelmed, and yet it seems you have plenty of time to look at people taking selfies, people pretending to be fairies— or whatever — when basically they just want someone to tell them how cute they are, and what has this world come to?

You tell me I'm overreacting even though I haven't said anything. You tell me I'm being ridiculous, that there's nothing to be concerned about, and a part of you is right. It's a waste of time to be concerned about the rest of the world when your own wife is hearing voices and calling all the neighbors to tell them about it—when she's got your children wrapped up in such blatant narcissism.

This isn't how it's supposed to be. This isn't how it's been. But you're falling down the rabbit hole, Kate, and we promised, we'd never be like the rest of them. This person I came home to, the one on the couch in sweats, wrapped up in other people and the garbage they spew out, this person isn't who you are. She isn't the girl I fell in love with. And the problem is, I don't know what I'm going to do about it. I only know that we can't go on like this.

≈

I'VE ALWAYS FOUND THAT DISTRACTION IS THE BEST WAY TO solve a problem, and it's how I plan to solve at least a few of ours.

"I ordered takeout for dinner," you say, watching on as I rummage through the refrigerator. It's a good thing, I note, surveying the bare shelves. Monique did the grocery shopping, and clearly all it takes is a few days for things to start slipping around here.

"Delivery?" I ask over the noise, the kids running circles around me. If you reply, I can't tell, because it's hard to hear over the noise level, and someone has taken someone's something, and suddenly all hell has broken loose.

"Yes," you yell, and clearly your hearing is better than mine. "The usual."

"Oh," I say and I close the refrigerator. "Actually, I have plans," I tell you, and we're yelling back and forth when yelling was something we said we'd never do. *Raise your words, not voice. It is rain that grows flowers, not thunder.* Rumi said that.

But you aren't thinking about Rumi or rain or flowers. You're a snake poised to strike. I can tell by the look you're giving me. It could kill, and apparently I was wrong before. You can fight in front of kids.

"Go play—" I tell them making sure my voice has a hard edge to it. Like their mother, they don't budge "Out of the kitchen—" I order. "Or I'm taking your iPads to work with me tomorrow." That's all it takes. All eyes are on me.

"Fine," they huff in unison, and I watch as they file out of the kitchen, taking their fight with them.

"Jude—" you say, and your voice is low, you're ready to attack. I cut you off.

"I know—" I start and I turn in your direction. "It's not ideal having to go out tonight… but I was thinking you could join me."

You cock your head and your expression changes. You weren't expecting that. "And what about the kids?"

"Ask Josie to watch them."

"I can't ask her again…" you say twisting your mouth, weighing your options.

"All right. We'll take them to Rudy's."

You scoff, and I'm not surprised. "Your father doesn't even like kids."

I lean against the kitchen counter, and then I take an apple from the bowl that's sitting on the island. "He'll be fine with them for a few hours," I counter, biting into it.

"That was for decoration," you chide, eyeing the apple in my mouth and it's clear you've softened.

"For who?'"

You pinch the bridge of your nose, and you don't respond. You're trying to be civil, but it takes a lot out of you.

You hop up on the kitchen counter, eyeing me suspiciously, but I can see that you're at least halfway sold on the whole Rudy thing. You let out a long sigh, and then you shake your head. "I'm going to have to hire a new nanny… I'm going stir crazy here, Jude."

I knew this was coming, and so I answer accordingly. "I can see that."

"I'm not sure I'm cut out for this full-time parenting gig…"

"You probably should have thought of that two kids ago," I reply, because if you think I'm afraid to play hardball you're wrong. I'm not okay with a part-time parent for my kids—so you're going to have to deal with it. "Suck it up buttercup, that's what my father always said."

You don't respond immediately. You stare off beyond my shoulder, and I don't know where you've gone, but I can feel it's somewhere very far away. "Give Rudy a call," you tell me as you hop off the counter. "I'll get dressed."

"Kate?" I say, just as you reach the door.

You turn back, brow furrowed.

"Do you know where we're going?"

"Of course," you say, and then you grin. You clap your hands just slightly, and I swear it's like you've just morphed into an entirely different person. You meet my gaze and the light in your eyes is back. "We're going to work."

MY FATHER IS NONE TOO PLEASED ABOUT THE IDEA OF babysitting, which I'd predicted. But what could he say when we show up unannounced? He couldn't exactly say no—not in front of them, and so here we are. Just the two of us skirting around issues, doing our best to play nice.

You stare out the window, and I wonder if it's a good time

to tell you about the trip. It's been raining on and off for the last few hours, but now it's as though the sky has opened up, and it is unleashing everything it has on us, every last drop. The darkness of night and the sound of the rain seem to have a calming effect on you, and I decide it's probably best to drive on in silence. I decide to let it be. You don't ask where we're going, in fact you don't speak at all, and I wonder what you're thinking. But I won't ask. You and I, we've never been the kind of couple who share our every thought, and I don't intend to start now.

By the time I pull over and park, a few blocks down from the bar, you've fallen asleep. I like you like this, peaceful and content, all mine, and I think I could stare forever.

Instead, I place my hand on your thigh. It startles you awake, and I swear you just about jump out of your skin.

"Easy there," I say, eyeing you up and down.

Your breath is ragged, and it takes you a few seconds to get ahold of yourself but eventually you do.

"I was dreaming," you say, using the back of your hand to wipe the drool from your cheek, and it's knowing the way a person looks when they first wake, knowing someone this intimately, that gets me every time. There's nothing quite like being this vulnerable. No one tells you there are levels to intimacy, so many levels, in fact, and just when you think you've gone as far as there is to go, you're always surprised to find there's more.

"Where are we?" you ask, and you glance from side to side, but rain drops smatter the windows, making it nearly impossible to see out.

"4th Street," I tell you.

You rub your eyes, and you know what that means. I don't have to explain it, and I realize how much I'd miss that if we can't find a way to make this work. Not that I want to think this way—it's just...well, you know me, and 'Plan B' is not something I like to go without. I study the curve of your tits as you sit up a little straighter in your seat, and I hope we give each other reasons to want to stay. The way your tits look in that shirt just might be enough.

You yawn and you stretch and your shirt lifts with your arms revealing just a hint of belly and maybe coming here was exactly what we needed. "Fourth Street," you say. "Hmmm. Well... it's a good thing I had a nap..."

"Let's run through the plan—" I say and I start to explain and it helps to see that I have your attention instantly. "But, first— I need you to promise me, Kate, and by that I mean swear to me, that you are going to follow directions this time. We don't need another situation on our hands."

You shift in your seat and you eyeball me. "Why did you ask me to come?"

"Because I want you here."

"Is that so?

I shrug. "You're here, aren't you?"

"Do you trust me Jude?" you ask, and it's amazing. You always know something's up, you always know when I'm holding something back. Nonetheless, it turns me on that you're so smart—that you know me this well. You're a mind-fuck, darling, and that's a beautiful thing to be.

"What kind of question is that?"

You close your eyes just briefly and then you shake your head. "Just answer it," you demand, and I love how I exasperate you. It's good to know the feeling is mutual.

"Of course, I trust you. You're my wife..."

You roll your neck. "Well, I'm not so sure..."

"I don't see how it's my job to convince you of anything."

I watch as you clench your teeth. It's your tell. You don't respond, at least not verbally. Instead, you cross your arms and you pout.

"All right," I finally relent. I tread carefully. You can lead a horse to water but you can't make 'em drink.

"All right, what?"

"All right, I'll prove it. I trust you enough to leave town tomorrow."

You do a double-take. "You're fucking kidding me, right?"

"In fact, I'm not."

You ball your fists and take a deep breath, and you're so transparent in your anger. "But tomorrow morning is kinder orientation. I've told you that a million times…"

I fold my lips, and then I smile, but just a little. Happy people add fuel to the fire of those who are not. Right now you're not the least bit happy, and that means I need to tread carefully. "My flight is in the afternoon."

"Yeah, well—it doesn't matter. You'll still be distracted…"

"I will not. I'll be the most non-distracted, most present father there." You roll your eyes at my response and you're still pouting. It isn't cute, so I take it a little further. "It's a promise."

You stare out the window, and we don't have time for this but what can I do? It is what it is. Plus, I understand the importance of telling you I have another trip before we make the kill—while I still have a carrot to dangle in front of you.

I make a show of checking my watch.

"Fine. Whatever," you relent. "Do what you need to do," you say, glancing over at me, even though you don't mean it at all.

I playfully breathe a sigh of relief, but you're not in the mood to play. Not yet.

"Now—what's the plan?" you ask, and your voice is hard. You're not giving in easily, and you want me to know it.

"I'm going to drop you here," I say, thumbing through my phone. When what I'm looking for pops up on the screen, I hand it to you. You glance at the photo, and you begin to flip through others. You know the drill; you know it's important to familiarize yourself with a place.

You lay the phone on your thigh as realization hits you. "You're not coming with me?"

No, I'm teaching you to fish, I think to myself. I don't say it though. "It's a small place."

You nod, and you want to be trusted. I'm good at giving you what you want.

"He usually sits at the end of the bar. To the right," I say, showing you his picture once again, just to be sure.

"What's this about?" you ask, biting your lip, and for some reason lately you always want to know. Before, you rarely asked my reason for anything. Before, a kill was a kill was a kill. Now, for some reason it matters.

"DUI—And I bet you a million to one he's driven himself here even though his license has been revoked…"

"DUI. Huh."

"Multiple," I tell you. "He did a stint in prison, got out, killed a woman and her unborn child and now he's awaiting trial…"

You check your appearance in the mirror. "It makes sense, he's drowning his sorrows," you say, and I've always loved your dark sarcasm. You glance at me then and your eyes cut holes in me. I want to believe that you've got this. I want to believe that *we've* got this. Not just the kill. But this marriage. This life. "You want me to pick him up…?" you ask, and you smile because you already know the answer. You just want to hear me say it.

"Yes. But on one condition. You have to convince him you're doing the driving. Make it non-negotiable. Whatever you have to do, I don't care, but he has to leave his truck where it is."

You jut out your bottom lip. "Okay."

"Tell him you're driving the two of you back to your

place, and then drive out to the barn. I'll wait in the back seat. He'll likely be too drunk to notice anyway."

"Why don't you just come in with me? Hang back," you suggest. "You know how much I like it when you watch me work…"

I shake my head slowly. You're a tease, and you make me smile. "This way no one sees the both of us."

"Yeah," you agree. "But what if someone sees *me?*"

"So?"

"So they'll think I'm trying to pick up other men. You know how people in this town talk…"

"This bar is a dump, Kate," I say and I laugh because I've forgotten how funny you can be when we're getting along. "I doubt you have to worry about anyone who knows us stepping foot inside a place like that."

"You'd better hope you're right," you reply, grabbing your purse. You open the door and you smile. Then you turn and you saunter away and your ass looks so good in those jeans that it takes everything in me not to follow.

~

YOU'RE IN THERE FOR WHAT FEELS LIKE FOREVER, AND I SEE IT for what it is, Kate, you're testing me. You want me to come to you, to see what you're up to, just like old times.

And I almost do. I'm getting antsy, just sitting here waiting. This isn't how I roll, and maybe I don't like this whole fishing thing after all. In fact, I'm just about to give up and go in after you—to take a risk we can't afford to take— when I see you walking back toward the car.

Alone.

You open the door, get in the drivers seat, and start the ignition. It takes you a second, but eventually you meet my eye in the rearview mirror.

You aren't saying anything, and I cock my head. "What the fuck?"

I study your expression, and I don't know what happened in there or why you've come out empty handed, but one thing is clear: you're pissed.

You swallow, and then you give me the death stare. "He's not into women, genius."

~

CHAPTER ELEVEN

KATE

I made a fool out of myself in that bar, and even if you didn't set me up intentionally, this isn't the end of it. I don't know when—or how—but I'll get you back. I can promise you that.

For now, I drive. At least, the rain has let up. The streets are dark and slick and desolate, and I swear it feels as though the whole world is against us. Not to mention, I heard my father's voice coming out of that bar, and that's impossible because he's dead. Things are changing Jude, they are. I feel the earth turning faster, I sense summer moving further and further away, and suddenly I feel like we need to squeeze every last drop of it before it's gone for good. Winter has never been good to us. Everything dies, and it's coming, it's turning colder, it always does.

Sure, there's something about the coming of fall that always makes me feel a bit down, even though it's winter I love most. There's something about the muted gray of each day that grips me and won't let go. And when it finally does, it's as though everything is right in the world, because you're finally seeing the truth of it all, in a way that's only possible when everything has been stripped away.

If my mood seems bleak, it is. I'm tired and I worked hard in there. You ask if I'm disappointed, and it's a stupid question. Of course, I'm disappointed. I'm disappointed about not getting the kill. But it's more than that, too. It's everything and it's piling up all at once.

THE AIR AROUND US IS THICK, IT'S FILLED WITH HUMIDITY AND unspoken words. Mostly, because you refuse to speak on the drive back to your father's which means nothing has been settled. I know you think I'm angry about you leaving town and so I won't tell you, my irritation was all an act. In truth, I'm happy you're going because quite frankly, I could use some space. I think *we* could use some space. A little breather will do us good. Also, it'll give me some time to get to the bottom of things without you breathing down my neck, questioning my every move. That's the thing about you I love most and at the same time it's the thing that bothers me more than anything. You want to control everything, including me, but I've never been one to be controlled.

Speaking of control, I'm certain I can keep the voices at bay if I can just stay busy. To help with that, we need a new nanny, and obviously securing one will be tough if you're around. You won't make this easy, and I don't have the energy to go about it the hard way. Not with everything else going on. You don't think we need help, and even if you did, well, you don't like people. Not just some people—it goes further than that. You don't like anyone, and I'm beginning to think I fall on your long list. I've never met a person who can find fault with people the way you do, but I've gotta hand it to you, it's impressive.

It's okay though. I have a plan, and you like plans. If I can just get the children handled, then I can do what it is I know I need to do to fix this— to fix you. I can find your mother. Because let's face it, Jude. You have mommy issues.

~

WHEN WE ARRIVE AT RUDY'S TO RETRIEVE THE KIDS BRADY IS waiting for us at the front door. "Livy is crying," he says matter of factly. "She can't find Pops."

"What do you mean she can't find him?" you ask scooting past him.

I search the house, trying to find Olivia. Eventually I spot her huddled in the kitchen her knees drawn up to her chest. "Where's Pops?" I ask touching her hair. It's immediately clear something isn't right here, the feeling is palpable.

"I think he's outside," Brady says and my breath catches. You waltz into the kitchen after checking the bedrooms and you meet my eye. "Outside?" you say and in three quick strides you're opening the back door. You look back at me briefly and I can see you're making a choice about whether to stay or go, but it really isn't a choice at all is it, and then you're gone.

I don't know who or what is out there but it seems I have a choice to make too and while I want to follow you out into the night, instead I stay with Olivia. I take her in my arms and I look at our son. "Brady," I say and he looks up from his iPad. "How long has Pops been outside?"

"Thirty-seven minutes," he tells me glancing back at his device.

I swallow hard. "And what happened before that? Why is Livy crying?"

"Because she's scared," he tells me without a hint of emotion. Brady isn't your average four year old, and sometimes that's hard to take. Like you, most things are either offered up without warning or have to be coaxed out. It's like charming a snake, and it isn't as easy as it looks.

"Brady," I say his name again, and I know he knows what I want even if he's hesitant to give it. *Like father, like son.*

I watch as he stands up and retrieves something from the kitchen counter. He walks over to me and hands me a box.

"Livy didn't like the man with the box."

I take it from his hands and I stand, ready to get you. Ready to tell you it isn't safe out there, that someone has been here and this is real. "What man?"

"The one who said to give you that," he tells me, nodding toward the box in my hands.

I take the box and I leave the room. I know it's time to find you. We meet haphazardly at the back door, nearly colliding with one another.

You gasp. "Jesus. Kate."

"How bad is it?" I ask, instantly reading your expression.

You look away. "I'm going to need your help getting him inside."

I clear my throat, needing you to give it to me straight. I raise my brow, and I wait. Your expression replies in kind, and it tells me everything I already knew. It's bad.

I crane my neck to try to see what we're dealing with, but it's pitch-black out. "He's unconscious," you say and you rub at your jaw. "But he's alive." It should make me feel better, but it doesn't. Because you and I both know that whoever was here didn't come here to kill your father. Otherwise he'd be dead. They came to send a message.

≈

I WATCH AS, SLOWLY AND METICULOUSLY, YOU GO FROM ROOM to room, gun cocked and ready. You're all stealth-like, checking everything: windows, and doors, in closets, under beds. It's amusing— we both know you aren't likely to find anything.

You give the all clear, and then you lead the kids into your father's room, where you tuck them in with those devices you hate so much. It feels ironic, although now does not seem like such a good time to point that out.

∼

DEATH I CAN DEAL WITH, IT'S THE LIVING THAT MAKE IT HARD. This is what I'm thinking as I stand over your father. "Is he gonna be okay?" I ask, because I want to know but also because I need answers to questions that I can't very well ask if he's dead.

"I think so."

"Should we call an ambulance?"

"No."

"Why not?" I ask, mostly because I need him to stay alive.

"He wouldn't want that…"

"So?"

"So, we have to be smart about this," you say. "Let me assess him in the light and we can go from there."

You shine your cell phone flashlight and it's the unnatural way his arm is twisted that catches my eye first. He's lying in an interesting position, face down in the dirt, as though someone placed him there, and he's so still, more still than I've ever seen him.

"Who did this?" I ask.

"I don't know," you tell me. "But I intend to find out."

∼

"WHAT'S IN THE BOX?" YOU DEMAND TO KNOW ONCE WE'VE

gotten Rudy inside. I think we should call for help but you're clearly still deciding.

"See for yourself," I tell you. It's easier that way.

"The man said to give it to you. To you and Daddy," Olivia says and I look up. I hadn't heard her come out of the bedroom. She's supposed to be asleep. At least she had been the last time I checked.

I swallow hard and I look over at you.

You're practically jumping down her throat in an instant, asking question after question. *What did this man look like? What was he wearing? How tall was he? What exactly did he say?*

"He just said to give it to you," she offers, her eyes tired.

"To me or to mommy?"

"To mommy. No—wait, he said... give it to your mommy *and* daddy."

She shakes her head. I can see that she feels your intensity, your need for her to get it right, and I can tell she's trying so hard for you, she really is. "I can't remember. I'm sorry," she finally says and I go to her.

"Think Olivia. You have to THINK," you say and you're practically shouting.

"Jude," I say and my tone isn't friendly. Not at all.

"He said to give it to mommy and daddy," Brady pipes in, and all eyes turn in his direction. I guess no one is sleeping tonight. "He was tall," he tells you. "Bigger than Pops, with brown hair and scary eyes. But he wasn't scary. He was..." he thinks for a moment, choosing his words carefully. "Kind of nice," he concludes thoughtfully.

We lock eyes, and I can see the fear in your expression.

You start to pace.

I peek inside the box, and then I close it quickly. You lead the children back to bed.

〜

It's four in the morning on a night that will never end.

"Did you call an ambulance yet?" I ask full well knowing the answer.

You shake your head. "He doesn't want me to."

"We could drive him. But that would mean waking the kids."

You don't respond.

I sigh. "Well, at least he's awake…"

"Yeah," you say, but you're a million miles away.

"What was he hit with?"

You look at me then. "A bat, he thinks."

"Dear God."

"Are you going to tell me what's in the box?" you ask and I know if you really wanted to know, you'd have already looked yourself. I hand it to you, and I watch your face as you open it.

You pull out the note and you read. You stare at it for so long I'm not sure what to think.

What does it say?" I ask. I haven't read it because I hadn't really wanted to know. Now I do.

You look over at me. "An eye for an eye."

"Well, I guess that explains the eyeball," I tell you and this time you don't look away.

~

CHAPTER TWELVE

JUDE

Between you and I, the two of us checked on the kids approximately every five seconds last night. Parenting doesn't stop when bad things happen. You don't get breaks just because you need them. Kids are demanding like that. Also, I had no idea I could find another reason to love you more. But I did. This whole situation with my father has caught me off guard—it hit too close to home. I can deal with bad cops and dead bodies and most things that come my way. But whoever is sending these notes is getting more brazen, first by showing up at Rudy's house, and second by interacting with our children. If they're trying to get their message across, and they are, I've got to figure out a way to let them know I got it. Whoever it is wants to have a conversation, but conversations aren't one-sided affairs and I've had enough of them doing all the talking. I'm ready to say my part.

You tell me I'm overreacting—but I know it's just your way of saving face. You say that if the person had wanted to hurt them, he would have. I don't agree. Not when it comes to my children. There are a lot of ways to hurt a person, and they aren't all immediate. You of all people should know that.

~

YOU DRESS THE KIDS IN THEIR SLEEP. IT'S NEARLY TEN O'CLOCK by the time we drag them out of bed. Kinder orientation is at eleven, and you're terrified we'll be late. I watch in amusement as you throw granola bars at them in the backseat and coach them about not telling anyone about Pops or what happened last night. This is a disaster waiting to happen, and this is why people shouldn't rush things. You tell me we have to go—that parenthood doesn't stop when the shit hits the fan—and it's funny how you're always in my head.

I stare at you in the passenger seat, and I can't believe we've come this far. Our little girl, the one we never thought we'd have, is starting school and despite not getting any sleep, you look better than ever. You look over at me, and I can't read you, the way you read me. Not right now, anyway. You're closed off, the way you sometimes get. I smell fear, but you don't dress the part. You're wearing jeans with heels, your hair's blown out, and you certainly don't look like a woman who stayed up all night staring at a person's eyeball mounted and deftly displayed inside of a box. *Where did it come from?* You kept asking. *Whose is it? Who would do this?*

Eventually, I got sick of your questions and I snapped at you. That's probably why you're not letting me in, why you've shut down. But the thing is, I don't know who did this. But what I do know is that whoever he is… he's careful, meticulous, and likely not a novice. Also, he clearly has a bone to pick with either one— or both— of us and it appears he likes to play. More importantly, if I knew who he was, I certainly wouldn't have sat there nursing my father or listening to your open-ended questions.

I would've been out there doing something about it.

~

"PEOPLE CAN'T STOP TALKING ABOUT YOUR PARTY," ONE OF THE dads, Ron, says, slapping me on the shoulder. He and a group of five other men join me, no doubt looking for respite from this bullshit our women dragged us into.

I smile politely but I don't offer the dignity of a response. I'm well aware he isn't referring to your spectacular hostess skills. You would have the perfect retort, but you're not here. You've taken the kids to drop them off in the classrooms they've designated to childcare while they syphon their weary parents off into the library and some people call this a break. Not me, I'm not nearly as enthusiastic about 'escaping my children' as the other dads seem to be. In fact, I'm not sure we should leave them at all, but this doesn't stop you. You're looking for a break, too.

I look around, and this is not what I'd call an escape. I'm surprised and yet I'm not. This school is massive, nothing like the elementary school I attended. But then, my parents were spared private school tuition. They tossed me into the public education system on a wing and a prayer, hoping I wouldn't be churned out like a factory worker—like the other poor bastards. The worst part was— it wasn't that they couldn't afford tuition to a nicer school, a better education, a better life— it's that they said they wanted me to learn to fend for myself. They wanted me to learn people skills. *No one's going to give you a free ride, my father always said. You've got to learn how to deal with people.* And yet, here I am, surrounded by a group of other men, none the wiser, not liking people any more or less than I did back then, and you know I hate these kinds of things.

"Just think," you say, sauntering up behind me, reading

my mind even though you can't see my face. "This is just the beginning," you inform me, handing over a Styrofoam cup. It's full to the brim with coffee, nearly spilling over, in fact. But you are careful. You turn, eyeing the men one by one. "Hello, gentlemen," you say, and you're quite the character and maybe my parents were wrong all along. Maybe it's that fancy private education your parents sprung for that makes you so appealing. Or maybe it's your tits and those eyes that are anything but innocent. I'm going with the latter.

"Did you guys see that game last night?" you ask, blowing on your coffee. You're a tease, and it irritates me that I'm equally amused and irritated. "Can you believe it?" you say and your voice comes out exasperated and I have no idea what you're talking about. I do, however, know for a fact you weren't watching any game, at least not any kind these men would have seen. It never ceases to amaze me what a good liar you are. But they like your lies, they get you—they know exactly which game you're referring to. I rub my face, and Jesus, Kate, why must you insist on engaging people? Why can't we just go to our seats and get this over with? I have other matters I need to attend to, and small talk isn't one of them. You smile at me, and you're doing that thing you do again, where you're reading my mind. And I don't know whether you're intentionally trying to piss me off, or if you just believe your own lies, but before I know it you're rattling off facts, and you're going back and forth about shit that is utterly meaningless, and why can't you see that you're trying to impress the wrong team? The women in this room are never going to like you if you keep chatting up their men—if you keep showing off.

You pause mid-sentence, and you finger the pearls around your neck and then you lower your voice. Your gaze follows. "Oh, and by the way... did any of you happen to hear a woman scream the night before last?"

I glance around at the men as one by one they rack their brains. They look from one to the other, wondering what to say.

"Can't say I did," Ron tells you, always eager to be heard.

"I'm a heavy sleeper," another admits when he realizes he won't be the odd one out.

"Could have been a coyote," the one with the belly adds.

"Yeah, maybe," you say. "But, you know," you add raising your brow and you go on but not before you've made a show of licking the rim of your coffee cup. "I'm pretty sure I heard what I heard…"

All eyes are on you until Stanley steps forward, "I heard it," he tells you, and you meet his eye, cocking your head to the side. Your face lights up because you like it when people agree with you even when they're full of shit.

"I couldn't sleep," he says, and I see something register on your face. A look passes between the two of you.

"Whew," you say, and you laugh just a little. "And here I thought I was losing it."

"It was odd," he tells you, and now everyone's looking at him. Especially me. He sips his coffee, and he's mirroring you and I don't like it. "But I'm sure it was nothing," he adds. "Otherwise we'd have already heard…"

"Yeah," you nod, and then you look over at me. You smile just a little, and you wear the expression of a woman who thinks she's gained something.

"Jude," he says, extending his hand out to me. "I didn't know you were going to show today."

"Stanley," I say, shaking his hand. "What is that supposed to mean?"

"Oh, you know, you're out of town so much," he says, and I eye him, waiting for him to elaborate, all the while I grip his hand harder.

"Looks like I touched a sore spot," he smirks. "Sorry, man.

I meant nothin' by it," he says as he removes his hand from my grip. I watch as he wipes it on his pants. It's not intentional; he just doesn't realize I'm watching this closely. That, or he doesn't care, and he needs to watch himself or I'll wipe that smirk off his face.

"Kate," he says, eyeing you. "Maybe we should start a neighborhood watch program... you know, give us insomniacs something to do."

You nod, and then you smile, and for the first time I'm glad I came. I had no idea this asshole was as clever as he thinks he is. Nor was I aware he knew so much about us.

～

"Kate," I whisper, pulling you aside. It's 'intermission' and who knew an orientation for kindergarten could be so hardcore? I mean they act like we're sending our child off to college—not somewhere to learn to color and play nice with people. At any rate, if she's anything like her mother, they'll certainly earn every penny of the inflated tuition they're charging. It's not that I'm cheap, and it's not that I don't want my children to get a good education. We've been over this. I just don't like this many rules. Not even when I pay good money for them.

"Why aren't you talking to the other moms?" I ask, looking around the room, hoping people leave us alone.

You shrug, and then you glance in their direction. You look back at me. "They don't like me."

"Bullshit."

You cock your head to the side, and you study my face, sizing me up, wondering what I'm getting at. "They blame me for what happened at the party..."

"So?"

You pick apart a donut, and stuff a piece into your mouth. "So— it's awkward."

"So, then— make it not awkward."

You swallow, and then you stuff the other half in your mouth. "How am I supposed to do that?" you ask, your mouth full.

I shake my head, and then I bring you in close so you can't overreact by what I'm about to tell you. I kiss your forehead. "By not holding the attention of their men."

Aware that we have eyes on us you eventually pull away. Your eyes meet mine. "I don't think that's the issue."

I smile at you and your naiveté. I can't help myself. "That's because you're not like them," I tell you. "And that, Kate, is your first problem."

∼

I CHECK ON THE KIDS. YOU GO FOR MORE REFRESHMENTS. When we get back to our table, I can tell you're irritated. If I had to guess the reason, I'd say it's probably because you hate it when I'm right.

You hand me the glass of orange juice you brought me even though you know I hate orange juice. I take it from you, and as I go to pull out your chair, you trip forward on your heel, spilling the contents of your glass down the front of your blouse. Your face suggests shock as it spills down the front of your shirt and all eyes are on you. Of course they are, because now your shirt is practically see through and this is not a wet t-shirt contest, this is our child's future. The men at the table all stand to help, while the women look around helplessly, as though they aren't a group of mothers with young children, as though they've never dealt with a spill in their life.

They nervously glance around at each other. I hand you a

stack of napkins. You blot at your sopping shirt and you frown and before I know it you're breaking down.

Even I'm amazed at your performance and although I try I can't recall the last time I saw you cry. I didn't know you had it in you, this level of emotion and I tell you what, it really is something to see.

"I'm sorry—" you sob, choking on tears. "I never do this... it's just that Jude's dad...well... he took a spill last night and we were up all night with him..." You blow your nose and then you wave your hand in the air. "You know just to make sure... old people and falls...well, you just never know."

Everyone looks around for help, as though some imaginary adult will come to the rescue and teach them how to handle people who lose their shit, people who aren't good with emotions. You dab at your blouse, and someone hands you a wet napkin, which you use to blow your nose, and my god you're a mess.

You don't stop there. You have stamina. "Anyway, if that weren't bad enough—his memory has been spotty for several months, and now they're saying it might be... you know..." You pause, your eyes wide, and wow, I don't know where this is coming from, but I'm mesmerized. You sniffle while you pretend to search for the right word. Then you dab at your eyes with your fingertips, trying to compose yourself. You don't quite make it all the way and so you go on. "Well I won't— I just can't go there. Plus, with Olivia starting school and all, well, it just feels like I can't keep up anymore..."

The women look at each other, one by one, and even I can see that they've softened just a little and you are brilliant. They get off on seeing that you aren't perfect after all. You have problems, real problems, and no doubt they're excited to dissect them behind your back. I rub your back, right where the knife will go in, of course it will, you've just handed it over and begged them to stab you with it. I offer you my seat and you take it. They offer looks of sympathy, so much as the Botox in their face will allow anyway, and you have made them feel with your performance. You're like a wounded bird, and these women, that's the kind they like best of all.

"Oh, Kate," one of them says. "I can't imagine. That has to be a lot to manage."

"Let us help," another chimes in. "That's what neighbors are for."

"I'll set up a meal calendar," the one named Sarah says, and if I remember correctly, aside from Josie, I think she's the only one of them you actually like.

You wipe at your eyelids once more, but you only manage to smudge your mascara more and damn that smokey eye looks good on you. You're probably wondering how I know what a 'smokey eye' is and it's because I see what you search on the internet.

As you clear your throat, I do the math in my head about how long it's been since we've fucked. I find it interesting how in the middle of all of this, you can find yourself missing a person, particularly one that's seated next to you. But you can.

"Oh, and Anne," you say, meeting her eye. "I was doing some reading the other day, and I came across an article on seizures, and then I decided to do a bit of research, you know, to make sure it was factual—you never know these days... Anyway, they say an extra dose of vitamin D can really help," you say, and you offer the slightest of smiles. "I meant to send you the article but I've just been so busy..."

"Seizure?" One of the women exclaims dramatically, and they all look to her.

"I had no idea!" another says. "Anne! How scary. Why didn't you say anything?"

She smiles, loving that the attention has fallen on her.

"Yes, well," she says patting her ridiculous updo. "I didn't want to alarm anyone."

"Are you kidding?" two of them murmur in unison, each annoyed at the other for beating them to the punch, and suddenly it's a free for all as to which insufferable woman can appear the most concerned.

She waves her hand in the air, halting the chaos. "Well, in any case, it's been settled. The doctors say occasionally these things just happen. They agree it was random and they don't foresee it happening again."

Everyone cheers and I swear it's a fucking moment we're having here. I raise the glass of orange juice I hate almost as much as I hate these people. "A toast," I say. "To Annie."

"To Anne," her husband Stanley says as he raises his glass. It's clear he's politely correcting me as though I didn't know she hates to be called that.

"To Anne," everyone toasts. Everyone but you, that is, because you're wearing the contents of your glass. You give me the side eye, and then as everyone sips their drink, you take the o.j. from my hand and down it. You're one-upping me, showing me you've got this, and I appreciate your show-manship.

"By the way, Kate, were you able to find a new nanny?" Anne asks when things have settled a bit, and I hate her. You're happy again, and she's always the one to pull the rug out from under you—always the one who knows the right thing to say to get under your skin. It seems she and Sharon here are in some sort of competition to see who can do you in first. "It sounds like you could really use some help," she adds, smiling sweetly.

You shake your head. "No, not yet."

"We know a girl," Stanley offers up.

Your eyes are on him in an instant, and now mine are too.

"Stanley and I have several girls—girls that might be able

to help you out." Anne says proudly. "In fact, we've decided to start a little side-gig," Anne adds, and she's good. She's pitching the group.

"Like a charity?" I ask, even though I know full well that's not what she means at all. It's a dig at her other work, the kind she dragged you into, the kind that helps no one but herself.

"No," her husband counters. "Like a staffing agency."

I look over at him and *who is* this joker?

He looks at you. "Anyway, we have this one, and she's the best. I can send you her info—if you want?"

"That would be lovely," you reply, and I study his hands as he fishes a business card from his suit pocket. I almost move to intercept it, but I stop myself. Sometimes, it's best to see how things play out.

~

WHEN THEY FINALLY RELEASE US AND WE'RE ON OUR WAY OUT, Anne grabs you and pulls you aside. She lowers her voice but I'm good at reading lips. Also, body language. She doesn't trust you, not one bit. "Why did you cover for me back there?"

"I don't know," you tell her. You little downplayer you. "I guess I just wanted to settle any bad blood between us," I hear you say, and fat chance at that happening. Her posture is defensive. But then, it always is.

She purses her lips. "Thank you," she offers eventually. She takes a deep breath in, but she doesn't let it out. Not all the way. "I don't know what happened," she swears. "I've never been a big drinker..."

"It happens," you say, and then you flash a smile that could kill.

"Not to me it doesn't," she tells you, and then she replies in kind with a look I think you both understand.

"Truce," you say, holding out your hand, and you don't realize it, but you're about to make a deal with the devil.

I can see the hesitancy in her expression as she slips her hand in yours. "Truce," she confirms, and dear God, the odds of this turning out well are slim to none. It shouldn't make me happy. But it does.

After all, a distracted Kate is a good Kate.

~

CHAPTER THIRTEEN

KATE

Anne and Stanley were kind enough to send over a girl named Sophia. I liked her so much initially that after interviewing her I hired her on the spot. I think you will be proud of my efforts this time. I printed off a list of questions from the internet having read an article entitled 'how to hire a nanny,' and we got through most of them. Although really, my mind was made up when she told me she cooks, combined with the fact that Brady took right to her. I've been worried that after the whole thing with our last nanny that starting over would be a bad idea. But he and I, we had a talk about it, and he said he understood that Mommy has to go to work, ridding the world of men and women who do bad things to children—things like locking them in dark closets overnight, or really any time they refuse to listen. But, also, things he's too young yet to understand.

I haven't told you about Monique and what she did. And I won't, not yet, because I know you'll only blame me for hiring help in the first place. I've asked Brady why he didn't tell me, and he said she told him that Olivia would have to go in the closet too, if he told anybody and that's the problem with you and our son. You're both pretty bad about taking people at face value.

~

ALREADY, FOUR HOURS INTO HAVING SOPHIA AROUND, THE house is somehow magically spic and span, your father has been fed, we have groceries, and I swear it's like one of those fairy godmothers appeared and sprinkled fairy dust all over the place. She's amazing, this girl. Which helps, because you don't know it yet, but you and I, we have plans tonight. Your mark, the one from the bar, the one who isn't into women but enjoys getting sloshed and taking innocent families out with his car. Well— I can tell you what he *is* into— and it just so happens to be picking up random men in bars. Not that I'm surprised. You probably won't be either. As a general rule people who engage in risky behavior typically don't segregate it to one area of their lives. But then, I'm sure you knew that.

~

I SURPRISE YOU WHEN I TELL YOU IT'S DATE NIGHT. YOU'RE not sure about leaving the kids, or your father, but you also don't want me going alone, and so in the end, after extra precautions are taken, you agree.

I drive you to the bar, the one on 4th that you swear is a dump. Little do you know you're about to find out. It's actually not so bad after all.

"Uh-uh," you say, looking at me as we pull up to the curb and I motion for you to get out. You read me instantly. You know exactly what I have planned and you're having none of it.

"Oh— so it was okay for *me?*"

"I'm not picking up a man in a bar, Kate," you say, shaking your head. "It's just not happening."

I laugh, and this only pisses you off more. But I can't help myself.

"Fine," I tell you once I've gotten it together. You study my face, wondering, and I can tell you're slightly interested in what I have up my sleeve. "But it's easy, I promise."

You look at me and slowly shake your head. Sometimes you just need a bit of nudging, and deep down I get the sense that you like my plans.

I grab a slip of paper from the console. "Go in, sit next to him, and slip him this piece of paper. Easy as pie."

I watch as you unfold the note. You recognize the address written on it, and you look up at me and you narrow your eyes. "You think he's just going to meet us there?"

I smile. I was expecting a bit of pushback. "That depends on whether or not he finds you attractive or not—"

"Funny," you say, and you glance toward the bar.

I shrug. "I guess we'd better hope you're his type..."

You look over and you shake your head, but I know you secretly like it when I toy with you. Eventually you sigh and then I watch as you get out of the car and head for the bar.

I'd like to follow. But I won't. You got this.

~

"Do you think he'll come?" I ask on the drive over. You're staring out the window, you're planning, running through everything in your mind, and I know you know the answer.

"I'm not sure," you say. "Maybe."

We pull into the lot adjacent to the dilapidated warehouse where the mark will hopefully be meeting us, if you've done your job properly. I stare up at the sky—it's humid out tonight, and cloudy, and something in the air makes it hard to breathe. Usually, I'm buzzing when I'm about to make a kill, but for some reason tonight feels different. I wonder for a moment if it's PMS, but no, it can't be, it's too soon for that. I've already been here once today to drop supplies and scope the place out, and I can't help but notice how different it looks in the dark. I tell you as much, and you seem amused that I'm so prepared—so amused that you pull me into the back seat, tear off my pants and show me your appreciation. I like making up this way. I like your enthusiasm. But I don't tell you that. Mostly because I'm trying hard not to remember that filthy cop, and the way his hands roamed my body, and you're rather handsy tonight and it isn't helping. I feel bad when I have to mentally check out, and it makes me sick to think of another man with you inside me, but if it makes you feel any better, you should know I was plotting his murder all the while. And I promise you one thing, it will be slow and painful and nothing at all like what we've just done in the backseat of your car.

~

OUR GUY SHOWS UP EARLY, AND WE LOST TRACK OF TIME, which means we have to backtrack our way into the building. In the end, it's all good. I sneak up on him, and I'm happy, because this means I get to try out my new stun gun—that asshole cop has inspired me, and what do you know, it actually works. You hang back, but I feel your eyes on me, and this time I don't want to let you down. I want to give you a show. I want to make it worth your while.

The plan is to subdue him, and then put a bullet in his head, but you know me, I've always enjoyed a little spontaneity.

"Help me get him to the chair," I say, and I can hear the reservation in your breathing.

But you need not worry. I don't like it in here. The place smells of piss and stale air and something I can't name. "I'll be quick," I promise, and I'm pleased that you do as you're asked. It must have been the quickie. Sex makes you more pliable, it always has.

You help me tie him to the chair, and the poor bastard is begging—pleading for his life in a way that his victims never got the chance to. I find his whining annoying, and so I dig into the supplies I left earlier, just in case. I rip off a piece of duct tape and slap it over his mouth. Silence is better. And I know how much you like it. Then, because I don't want him to be too comfortable, I place a clothespin on his nose. His eyes bulge out of his head and I don't know why he can't find gratitude in his heart. He should consider himself lucky that he can't smell anything, because now I realize what it is I smell, and he should be glad he doesn't have to inhale the rat-infested air in this place.

You watch me suspiciously, toying with your gun. You're waiting for me to slip up, but I won't. You won't be disappointed. I'm making a comeback. On the other hand, our guy isn't so sure. His eyes are wide, and he shakes his head wildly from side to side as though this is all a bad dream, one in which he might wake up from if only he shakes hard enough. I stun him once more, this time placing the device directly to his neck, and this gives a whole new meaning to the electric chair. The voltage is not enough to kill, however, which is really too bad.

It does the job though, so I can't complain. Also, I can't help but notice the way his head just hangs there and I watch as just below the tape a trail of saliva escapes.

"You know," I say looking at you and then back at this asshole. "I think I have to agree...you're right. We live in a nation of pussies and the punishment *really* should fit the crime. And, yet, it almost never does."

I watch his face as I speak and he has calmed, he's interested in learning of his fate. I take a deep breath in and I let it out. I always did enjoy a bit of suspense. "If it did— you know—if things were different... if drinking yourself into oblivion and then getting behind the wheel of a car earned one more than a slap on the wrist... then I'd be willing to bet that woman and her unborn baby would still be around."

You watch me as you empty your gun and reload it and I know you. It's all for show. You hate that I like to drag these things out. You don't think it makes any difference when the ending is all the same and *that* is where we differ, you and I.

"Anyway," I go on, ignoring your unspoken demands that I get on with it. "If the punishment fit the crime...then you wouldn't have to spend so much time away from your own family hunting down bad guys like this piece of shit."

You look up at me then. "That's probably true."

Now that I have your full attention, I stick my finger in his eye, I give it a good poke. I want him to feel something and because there's nothing he can do about it, his hands are tied and there's no pain like eye pain. It's not satisfying enough though, and I remove the knife from my pocket. I flip open the blade, and he shakes his head. He moans against the tape. "An eye for an eye," I say, and it feels good putting my silent rage to good use.

I walk around him once, and I can see that he's close to hyperventilating. He's reached the point where he no longer cares what I have to say. Now, he's looking for a way out. Only there isn't one. Not for him. Of course, he already knows this, but survival instinct is a powerful thing. It's the same reason he drinks.

I clear my throat; I'm ready to deliver. "But alas, we do not live in a society that values justice," I say, and you meet my gaze and you offer me the same look you give when we're shopping and you're ready to go. "And therefore it's a good thing there are people like us…"

He starts moaning now and he wants to speak and so I rip off the tape slowly and then at once. He gasps for air for what feels like forever. You cross your arms. I wait.

"Please," he begs once he's gotten his fill of oxygen.

"Please," I exhale, throwing up my hands. I meet the eye he has left. "Now that's an interesting word, please."

"I'll do—" he starts, but he reeks of alcohol and desperation and so I cut him off. If he'd had even an ounce of that kind of self-control before, we wouldn't be here now.

"I bet the man—the one whose wife and baby you killed— I bet he knows that word well. Please."

He's not sure where I'm going, and I find it's always the best way.

"Just put a bullet in him and be done with it," you order, and it comes out as it should. It's a warning. Your patience is wearing thinner by the minute.

"Wait," he says. "I remember you. You're that woman, the one from the bar," he exclaims as recognition takes over. He pauses for a moment, and he's putting it all together. "Is this because I'm gay?"

I nearly choke on my laugh. "Are you kidding? I love gay people," I say, once I backhand him. I am many things, but a bigot isn't one of them. Also, he needs some sense smacked into him. "On the other hand, what I don't love are drunks who get behind the wheel of their vehicles and kill people because they're too selfish to kick back and enjoy a six-pack at home."

"Please," he pleads again.

"Do you know what the man whose family you murdered said when he found out they were gone? I do." I swallow. "I read the psych reports. Have you?

He looks at me, and he's not sure what to say.

"I didn't think so," I tell him. "Let me fill you in…"

"I'm sorry," he sobs. "I'll do whatever you want."

"Okay, then, well—this is what he said…He said, 'please don't let it be true. Please don't take her. Take me instead. Please don't let my baby die. Please. Please. Please.' He said that over and over and over. Until they had to medicate him. And you know what else? I'd be willing to bet he still takes that medication to help him sleep at night. Whereas you—you seem to have no problem."

"I swear I'll—"

I backhand him once again, because he doesn't deserve to get to beg after he's taken so much. I grab a fistful of his hair, and I yank his head backward toward me.

"Kate," you say, and you're telling me to pull the trigger, but I won't. Not yet.

"Please. It didn't work for him. Did you really think it would work for you?" I ask, dropping his head. He lets it hang, probably because he knows he's lost the battle. Some people fight to the very end, but you'd be surprised by how many don't. I take the roll of tape, rip off a piece and place it over his mouth.

"Do you have children?" I ask. He doesn't respond to my question which is ok because I already know the answer. He lives with his mother; she's likely the only person who'll miss him when he's gone. Or maybe she'll be glad to be rid of him —even if she'd never admit it, and you never know, it could go either way.

"The people you killed. That baby—his name was Samuel. His mother's name was Marie. The man, the one who lived, but not really…his name is Adam. You took a man and stripped his whole life away…"

Blood drips from the hollow cavity in his head where his eye used to be. His expression is pitiful. His lip quivers, tears spill out onto his face, but they're not the kind I want. They're not signs of guilt, but of self-preservation, and monsters like him who hide in plain sight are the worst kind.

He made a choice, and it's clear he hasn't learned his lesson. That family he killed—it could be ours. Sociopaths like him don't deserve a quick death, and that's exactly why I go against your order to put a bullet in him, and slit his throat instead.

~

YOU'RE ON MY ASS IN A MATTER OF SECONDS PRYING THE KNIFE from my hands. You eye his severed neck and then me. "Jesus, Kate. What the fuck have you done?"

I study the blood splatter and it is amazing. It's so vibrant and so messy just like all those emotions he brought out in me.

"This isn't very well going to go over as a suicide *now*..." you say as you motion toward his corpse, and I can see you're wracking your brain as to what to do about it. It's not that you didn't know all along. You knew almost from the beginning, and you certainly knew when his eye came out. I think you just wanted to see how far I'd go, and now you have your answer. I can go further. Just wait and see.

I shrug and I admit, though not out loud, that I've been so busy I hadn't quite thought the disposal part through. Or much cared. Dead bodies have a way of taking care of themselves, if you give them enough time. It's the bones that give you away. Bones tell stories. But you know this.

I consider you for a minute or two, but mostly I stare at all that blood. It's funny what makes up a person. Eventually, I shrug. "So we take him with us..."

You deadpan. "I don't want to take him with us."

"Fine," I tell you, and then I hastily gather my belongings. "Suit yourself."

You surprise me when you don't load the body. You don't agree with me, and you don't ask for my help. You leave him there, and I don't know what your plan is, but it had better be good.

~

AT FOUR IN THE MORNING I AM AWAKENED WHEN YOU SLIP OUT of bed. If I weren't so tired, if you weren't still angry with me, and if it weren't Olivia's first day of kindergarten, I would follow. But all of those things apply in this situation, and it isn't until later over breakfast, as you tell the kids about the three alarm fire over in the warehouse district, that I realize how good at planning you are.

~

YOU'RE STILL NOT SPEAKING TO ME WHEN WE WALK OLIVIA into her first day of school, but we go hand in hand, and we look so perfect it's irrefutable.

"Jude, Kate," one of the other moms calls after us on our way out. We turn and we smile, and I watch as her face lights up when she looks at you. "You two *are* coming, right?"

I look to you. You're already looking at me. "Coming?"

"To Anne and Stanley's...they're hosting brunch for all the kinder parents in the neighborhood," she professes, and her face is surprised, almost taken aback. Like this is something we should have known.

Her eyes remain steady on you. "Anne said she told you."

You act surprised, but your memory isn't that bad and distracted. I'm trying to figure whose mother, whose wife she is, but I can't put my finger on it. "Oh. Right. It must have slipped my mind," you say to her, and then you look at me.

"But not mine," I confess and I make sure my face lights up like a Christmas tree when I look over at you. "Of course we're coming," I tell her. "We wouldn't miss it for the world."

You squeeze my hand so tight it turns blue.

~

CHAPTER FOURTEEN

JUDE

I can't afford to leave town. But I can't afford not to, either. You're a ticking time bomb. You're off your rocker, and you don't realize it, but you're going to get us both caught. Which is why, in the end, I cancel the trip. And here's the thing about that Kate, I love you— but I can't let you take us both down. It's so back and forth with you and me lately. One minute we're fine, and the next we're fighting. I have to admit, lately I miss being alone. I miss not having anyone to be responsible for. I miss not having such a liability on my hands.

Between nearly severing a man's head in that warehouse, and hiring help without my permission, something has to give. You're becoming more and more of a liability, and you know me, liabilities aren't my style. Now, I've got this dead bastard in the back of my trunk, and I have to do something about him. I set the fire—not to burn him as you assumed, but in order to destroy the evidence of the murder. You're so wrapped up in yourself that you think I handled it for you only you're in for a surprise.

But it gets better. The next thing I know, you're forcing

me to go to this brunch with you, even though I tell you I'm going to have to skip out early. I'm hoping you'll say never mind—that you'll offer me a pass— but you don't. And it only goes downhill from there. After we arrive you let those women lead you off to the kitchen, and you go willingly. I'm here for you—to be with you—but the men, several of the kids, and I, have been banished to the living room like it's some sort of speed dating bullshit event where we're thrown in the deep end to see whether or not we can swim. I don't want to make small talk; I've got better things to do than partake in a playdate for grown men—more important things—things like dealing with another body. Thanks to you. I could have made it look like a robbery, an OD, anything but what it was. Torture.

We used to be happy, Kate. Now it's fleeting. If I look hard enough every once in a while, I catch glimpses of that happiness but it doesn't come easy. You think I'm the kind of guy you can toy with, like I'm some fucking puppet on a string because I put a ring on your finger, but that's where you're wrong.

I'm here, for now, but if I were you, I wouldn't count on it remaining that way. Also, this house, this neighborhood, these people, they're ridiculous. Thankfully, I have Brady in tow, it helps; at least this way I don't have to talk to people, to avoid it I just pretend to be busy with him. It's pretty sad when you'd rather talk to a four year old than your neighbors, and that should tell you how bad it is. I have nothing in common with these people. They drone on about sports and their jobs and literal shit, all of it I could care less about. At some point Brady wanders off, I assume to find you or the bathroom, and my morale falls to an all-time low when I'm forced into meaningless chitchat. I can't handle much though, not today, and I'm looking for a way out when I say I'd better go in search of Brady. It isn't easy to get away, there are people looking to cling at every turn, but eventually, I find him. He's with Sam, Anne and Stanley's son, in the second living area, hiding off behind the curtains. This house is as ridiculous as the people who occupy it, everything that isn't white, is black, and it's making me dizzy. When I spot Brady, his eyes are wide, and so I peer around the curtains, and that's when I see that the other little boy's face is beet red. As I lean in to get a better look—it's dark back there in that corner, the perfect hiding spot— I realize that his face is not only red, but that it's rapidly turning blue. Within seconds he's clutching his neck. He doubles over, and that's when I haul him up by his armpits, position him appropriately and perform the Heimlich maneuver. I know a lot of things. But this isn't one of them, and that probably explains why nothing happens. He's squirming, panicking, and I'm doing my best to hold him in place, but he's little and slippery and he isn't making it easy. I can hear that people are starting to gather around no doubt wondering what in the fuck I'm doing to this kid, and I've never much cared for being the center of attention but I can't very well let the kid choke to death. Someone says to call 9-1-1, and before it comes to that, I give another attempt my best shot. Again, nothing happens. The third time had better prove to be the charm, otherwise this kid is going to die, and I don't lose, not in situations where it matters. I take a deep breath and then I press into his abdomen, harder than before, and with a quick upward thrust out pops a small red object. I watch as it shoots across the room, rolling across the floor. The little boy gasps, and then when he starts crying I exhale, and I realize I've never been more grateful to hear a child cry.

∽

PEOPLE ARE SURROUNDING ME, WHEN ALL I WANT IS YOU.

Brady is staring at me in shock. The boy is sobbing, and someone, I don't even know who, takes him from my hands. "You're a hero," one of the fathers says, slapping me on the back.

"A life saver," a woman says. By this point, you and those dreadful 'friends' of yours have filed in from the kitchen and are hovering, and the next thing I know people are clapping and patting me on the back, and I realize maybe it's not so bad to be liked after all.

$\sim$

"WE NEED TO TALK," YOU SAY, PULLING ME INTO THE bathroom.

I think you're going to offer me a quickie, something to make this whole thing worthwhile, and well, to be frank, after all those accolades I'm feeling up for it. My mood has shifted, and maybe you were right. Maybe I was meant to be here. Only you surprise me when you lean against the wall and cross your arms. You keep your legs closed, and this is the disappointing part.

"What?" I ask, and I don't know how you can be angry when your husband is a hero, a life saver, but I have to hand it to you, you have your ways.

You press your lips together. "Where was Brady when that boy was choking?"

I check my reflection in the mirror. You exhaust me, but heroes can't get tired and so I continue on. "What do you mean?"

"I mean, where was Brady?" you say, and you repeat the same question again, this time through gritted teeth. "Were you watching him?"

"Of course I was watching him."

You shake your head, uncross your arms and cross them

once again. "Of course," you say, but you don't mean it. "Was he near the boy or not?"

I furrow my brow. "Yeah, so?"

"So—there's something you should know about that…"

"What?"

"Brady pushed Monique."

I hear your words, and yet I don't. "He what?"

"It was Brady who pushed Monique down the stairs… I think he does bad things when he's angry, Jude. And what's worse is— I think it's becoming a habit."

I shake my head, trying to understand, trying to let what you're saying really sink in. "Why are you just now telling me this?"

"I tried," you say, and I'm not convinced.

"Not hard enough. Obviously."

You look at me and your expression is intense. "What are we going to do?"

"We have no evidence this is Brady's fault," I say, and even heroes don't have all the answers.

You look away and then back at me. "We have no evidence it isn't."

I check my watch. "We'll discuss this later," I tell you. "I have a meeting."

"Of course you do."

I turn to go but you scoff the second my hand clutches the door handle. "So that's it?"

I shrug, and I don't know what else there is to say. I'm tired of fighting, Kate.

Also, you lied.

～

I WALK HOME, LEAVING YOU AT THE PARTY. IF I DON'T HURRY, I'm going to be late for my meeting. It's warm out, and by the time I reach our house I don't have time for a shower, even though I'm drenched in sweat. Also, given the body that's in the trunk of my car and temperature outside, I don't want to take any chances, and so I take the spare car we kept for the nanny. I'm meeting my guy at that little diner, the one I took you to out in the country, back when we were first dating.

It turns out I arrive after he does, and you know how much I hate that. Even so, being here now, I have to say makes me a little nostalgic, it makes me long for a time when things were simple. I don't like feeling like this. I'm not in a good place and I need to be. Especially for this. Instead, I'm on edge, because of the brunch, but mostly because I'm here to meet the competition in order to offer him a job—a job that was supposed to be mine.

The diner, it's packed, it always is, and I find him seated in the only booth available, even though the waitress hasn't had a chance to clear it. He motions me to sit, and I order another cup of joe even though it's all for show, I have no intention of drinking it. I don't like substances that are addictive. At least not normally. But today doesn't feel very normal, and anyway that isn't the point. The point is when I arrive, my competition doesn't see a hero at all. He doesn't see a man who just saved a boy's life. He sees a man with problems, a man who's dragging, and I get what he's thinking, because I've seen it a million times myself in other men. *Don't ever let me become that, I used to say.*

"Everything okay?" he asks, looking up from the menu once he's decided on his order.

"Everything's great," I lie.

"Come on," he says.

I don't say anything.

"Trouble in paradise?" he asks.

I cock my head and wait him out.

"With your woman?"

"Ah, no." I tell him, and I manage a small laugh, even though his lack of manners perturbs me. I can't let it show.

"Huh," he says, studying me closely. He isn't buying my answer. "Well, at any rate, you look exhausted, man."

"Yeah," I tell him. "I mean—no—there's no trouble. It's just the kids...you know how it is," I sigh, and I touch the rim of my cup. "They're up several times throughout the night," I confess, even though it's you who's causing the trouble he's referring to, but then, I've gotten good at covering your ass.

"Well, sort of. But not really, to tell you the truth. My wife always dealt with that."

I force another smile. "Kate's pretty good about it—but you know, she gets tired sometimes, too."

"Yeah," he says, taking a sip of his coffee. "But women are built for that kind of shit," he adds, and if only that coffee were hot enough to burn his mouth.

"I guess," I say, over the small talk. I'm ready to cut to the chase.

He, however, apparently isn't. "You think our fathers were up at night? You think they were changing diapers and wiping mouths? No. I'll tell you what they were doing: they were working their asses off to put food on the table—they were going to war. They were the kind of men that made this country great. Now, look at us. We've got men thinkin' they need twelve weeks leave because their wife popped out a kid. We've become a nation of sissies. No one knows what their roles are anymore. It's disgusting, to be quite frank. And my God, this whole gender thing you hear about on the news. Men becoming women and shit. I tell you—I think our whole country is having an identity crisis. We've forgotten what it meant to be great. We're weak, and you don't even want to get me started on all of that politically correct mumbo jumbo they're spewing out these days..."

No, I don't. I don't bait him though. "That's an interesting perspective," I tell him instead. He's about to cover my ass, and now is not the time to disagree, even though I want to. The thing is, with people like him, it wouldn't matter anyhow. His mind's already made up, and trying to convince anyone of anything is an utter waste of time. That's what my mother used to tell me, anyway. Actually, on the subject of my mother... I've been thinking about her a lot. It started when I checked your phone and I came across your notes. You're trying to find her. But you won't. I know—I looked once. A long time ago. It's best to let sleeping dogs lie, Kate. I don't know why you can't just let things be, and that's another conversation I'm not looking forward to.

"Hey," I hear him say over my thoughts. "Hey, you," he calls tapping on the table.

I look up and shake my head.

"Boy, it's a good thing you've got me handling this mess for you. You's practically fallin' asleep here at the table," he says, and then he lets out a belly laugh that won't quit. Only he isn't laughing with me. He's laughing at me. I'm not a hero, Kate. I'm a joke. I'm handing my job and my money over to this illiterate bigot, and what in the hell was I thinking?

"Yes," I say and it kills me, those three letters.

"Well, while you was a dozin', I was talkin' about your wife... you know," he pauses for a second to stuff his mouth and then continues despite the fact that his mouth is full of biscuit. "I get how hard it can be managing it all with little ones," he swallows. "Okay—" he adds making sure I don't have the opportunity to cut him off. "Well, actually, that's a lie. I can't...because my wife did all that. But anyway, have you ever given any thought to coming to work for us?"

And there it is, the offer I was waiting for. I narrow my brow. "Us?"

"The firm."

I knew what he was referring to, but I wanted to make him say it.

I shrug. "I kind of like being on my own."

He takes a swig of coffee. "But you're here, aren't you..."

"It's just a one off thing," I say. "There's something else I have to take care of here in town." I picture that cop in my head, and it pisses me off as much as the asshole that's seated opposite me. "But if it's a problem—" I say. "I could always call someone else next time. I don't want to put you out," I say, reminding him that I'm doing him a favor as well.

"I hear you," he replies. "But if you change your mind," he says, as he rifles through his wallet. "Here's my wife's card. Give her a call."

I raise my brow. I hadn't expected this.

"She's a psychotherapist. All new hires have to go through her first."

I study the card. "I see."

"You seem pretty sound. And sure— I've known you for awhile. But how well can you really ever know a person, you know?"

I shrug, but he's right. You can't.

"Oh, and about your wife...I was sayin'...if you want to get her to step up a little..." he starts and then he lowers his voice so much that I have to lean in to hear the rest. "I'll tell you how to do it."

I feign interest, and I can't wait to hear.

"You gotta make her think she has a little competition."

I stick out my bottom lip just slightly. He's a goddamned genius, this one. Seriously? That's his advice? If he only knew the level of crazy I have to deal with.

"And this works for you?" I ask.

"Of course," he says, not missing a beat. "It's why I'm still married after nearly thirty years."

"Huh," I tell him, downing my coffee. "Maybe I'll give it a try."

"I'm tellin' you son," he chuckles, and I am not his son. "Let 'er think there's another woman in the picture. A real pretty one, to boot. You know, just look. Don't touch. But make damn sure she sees." He laughs so loudly it causes him to choke, and the people next to us stare. "I ain't lyin', he adds when he finally gets ahold of himself. "It works wonders."

I smile and then I pay the tab. I hand over his money for the job, and all of a sudden I need a nap. But mostly, it irritates me that I can't help but wonder if this asshole might have the answer I've been looking for.

∾

CHAPTER FIFTEEN

KATE

The nanny was supposed to have the day off, but I had her come in anyway. I have no idea how long you're going to be gone, but given that your father is still here, and you're worried about those letters, I'm betting it won't be long. Which means I have a lot of work to do in a short amount of time. My to-do list is pretty straightforward, but I write it out anyway just to see it on paper.

1. Find the cop. Take care of the situation.
2. Figure out who is sending us those messages. Take care of the situation.
3. Find your mother. Fix you.

I've been reading one of those self-help books about setting goals and fulfilling your life's purpose, and I'm starting to see the importance of having a plan. Sticking to it has always been more my issue, but I think you'll be happy to know that I'm working on it. I re-read the list, rethinking each item, just to make sure. Items one and two are pretty obvious. I think we would even agree on as much. The third, however, if I were to tell you about it, which I won't, you will say is a waste of time. It's okay, some things are better left as a surprise. Speaking of surprises, I learn something new everyday. The more I think about it, the more I realize that we're having all of these relationship issues because you've never healed the relationship with your mother. At least, that's what I read, anyway. Those women, our neighbors, they think I don't read but they're wrong. I just can't tell them what. I can't tell them I devour books like candy, books about how to heal you—about how to fix your mommy issues. And you know what those books say? They say you'll never let me in, that you'll never let me close, until you process your emotions toward her. I'll admit, at first I thought it was all psycho-babble bullshit. But that was before we started having all of these 'marital issues' and well, now I can't help but think it's all related.

But first things first. I've got to take care of that cop. I've gotta make the nightmares stop. It should be easy finding him. I remember that night clearly, I remember staring at the name sewn into that bastard's uniform, and I clearly remember what it said. *Officer Diggs. How fitting.* I called the station, but I didn't really get anywhere. It wasn't surprising. Because I know when you want to find something, it's best to just go after it directly.

≈

I DRESS FOR THE OCCASION IN RIPPED JEANS, A T-SHIRT, AND AN old ball cap, which I think belongs to you. As I slip it on, I can't help but notice it smells like you, and when I inhale it suddenly it hits me like a freight train. It's funny the effect a person's scent can have, how it can fuck you up, how it can make me *feel*. All of a sudden, you feel so far away, and I know we have to fix this. I know I want to. Sometimes I wonder. But not now. Now, I have a plan.

It's interesting how fast all of those good feelings instantly go to shit when I go to the garage and find that you've taken the nanny's car. This means I have to leave mine with her on account of the car seats, and drive yours instead.

I find the silver lining though, because your car is both cleaner and faster than mine, and I wonder if I've ever told you why I'm so good at silver linings. I don't think I have, and this is good, because it's nice to keep a little mystery in a relationship.

On my drive out, I mostly think of you, of all the times we've driven this road over the years on the way to our spot, the one down by the water. I know it was you and your first girlfriend's spot first, that it's her burial ground, but that's also what makes it sacred. I've been thinking about her a lot, about the connection the person who attacked me had, and I think I'm finally ready for answers. I've been avoiding that, avoiding the truth, because it reminds me of all that was lost, and we can't always have all the answers at once, can we?

Eventually, I pass the small diner you took me to on one of our early dates and it's packed. It always is. I've always loved that place, and I wonder if you remember that date. I can't help but recall how happy we were back then, and my reminiscing makes me consider stopping in for lunch. I don't though. I drive on because I've already timed this excursion, and if I'm lucky, and quick, I know I'll be able to make it back by the time Olivia arrives home from her first day of school.

I pull off the road and check the time, just to make sure. I park in that little spot beneath that old oak, the one I always point out whenever we come out this way. The sun overhead is beating against the pavement, and it's mesmerizing. Eventually, I kill the ignition, and I get out. It's hot out today, and I can't help but enjoy the intensity of it. It isn't long before I can feel the sweat beading up around my lower back. I walk around to the side of the car where I deflate the rear passenger tire just a little. I stand there for a few moments, mapping it out in my mind, and then I make the call. I'm not certain it will be Officer Diggs who responds, but I *am* certain I've got a fifty-fifty shot, and those are odds I'll take. In any case, even if it isn't him who shows, I'll get the information I need.

But when I see the squad car coming my way, I realize that luck happens to be in my favor today. When I see the cruiser pull up, it's the number on it that catches my eye first, and it's a match. *Bingo.*

～

I CAN TELL HE DOESN'T RECOGNIZE ME AT FIRST. IT COULD BE the blinding sun, or it could be the ball cap, but whatever the case, it's good news. I take a deep breath as he gets out of his car and starts in my direction. My pulse is pounding in my ears, and I almost have second thoughts. He leaves the driver's door open and walks around to the side of your car. My mind flashes back to that night, back to his hands on my body, and instantly I refocus on the task at hand. I know just what I have to do.

"Which one is it?" he asks, squinting into the sun.

"That one," I point, careful not to get too close.

I watch as he bends down to inspect the tire.

"You got a spare?"

"I think so," I say, sounding more unsure than I am, and doesn't every car have a spare?

He eyes me, and then his expression changes. I see something in it, it's as though he knows me from somewhere and I realize it's now or never.

He surprises me when he shakes his head and motions toward the car. "Pop the trunk. I'll grab the jack."

I press the button on your keys, and stuff them back in my pocket. I hold my breath and ready myself as he walks around to the back of the car. Moving quickly I reach for the stun gun I have stuffed in the back of my jeans and it's damp with sweat.

I hear his feet as they shuffle, and I hear him audibly swallow. I make my way around to the back of the car, careful not to make any sudden movement.

"What in the fuck?" I hear him say. I'm standing just behind him.

He reaches up and presses the button on his radio and that's when I see what he sees. The warehouse guy is lying there, wrapped in plastic in your trunk, and what the fuck is exactly right.

∼

CHAPTER SIXTEEN

JUDE

I 'm on my way home, feeling rather uplifted after having taken care of business, also a little Hendrix on the radio helps, when off to the side of the road I spot my car. Upon closer inspection, I see you and that cop, and Jesus, Kate, what are you thinking? I'm just annoyed enough that you've gotten to him first that I almost don't stop, but in the end, considering the body that's in the trunk, I can't help myself. When I pull off, I can see the two of you standing there, peering into the trunk, and then I watch as his knees buckle.

I get out of my car and rush to your side, and fuck, we're in broad daylight, and any passerby can see what's happening here. You are nuts, and that's when I know, this is over. This, being me and you, this family we've created, everything. Over.

"Help me get him into the trunk," you say. You're panting, and trying your darnedest against his weight to shove him in.

"What in the fuck?" I say, and you look at me, wild-eyed and on fire, you live for this kind of danger. I remove his gun and his pepper spray, and finally I cut his radio. You watch on in disbelief at how fast I can make things happen, and you have no idea. You're pleased I'm doing as you ask, but at this point what else can I do?

~

WE DRIVE HIM OUT TO THE WATER BECAUSE IT'S CLOSE, AND because we can't exactly take him home. I follow you in my car and you drive, slow and not at all steady, and I'm panicking on the inside but I refuse to let it show. I dial your cell. You don't pick up, and I'm annoyed that I have to try again at a time like this. I press your name again, and right when I think you aren't going to answer you do.

"You have to kill it," I tell you.

"What?"

"Go with it," I say, and there's a hard edge in my voice. I won't take the chance that this call is being monitored. They all are.

You laugh even though nothing is funny. Nothing at all. "*We* have to kill it."

"There *is* no *we* here, Kate."

You sigh, but you don't reply.

"You did this," I say, well aware that you can hear the venom in my tone, and I don't know why I'm so mad but I can't help myself. It's not that I wasn't going to kill him myself, it's just that you beat me to it, and I wouldn't have planned it like this. "You're going to handle it," I tell you.

"Fine," you say, and you hang up in my ear.

~

I SIT BACK AND WATCH AS YOU POINT THE .45 AT HIM, ordering him out of the trunk slowly. I'm not going to kill the guy, even though I want to. But it doesn't matter, does it?

I'm an accomplice. You got me into this and I keep my hand on my gun but mostly I sit back and watch you.

"That's it," you say as he steps out of the trunk. His legs are wobbly and he's clearly in shock. "Have you ever seen a dead body? Up close?" you ask, and he eyes you, not sure what to say.

He has now, I think, and apparently he isn't moving fast enough for you because you tell him to get back in.

"No," he begs. "I'll do as you say...I promise," he tells you, holding up his hands, and he's not in a position to be making promises.

You shift your stance, and you take aim. He cowers. "Sometimes you fuck with the wrong people," you say to him. "And sometimes it catches up with you."

He flinches and covers his head, and he's a cop, he should know better. They always do this, this duck and cover thing, and I've never quite understood it myself. Your arms aren't going to stop a bullet.

"Make it quick, Kate," I warn. "We have dinner plans."

You glance at me, and the last part was a lie, but something in it got your attention.

"No, wait!" he begs, and he's pissed himself. He's literally pissed himself. As I watch urine trickle down the legs of his brown trousers, I want to beat the shit out of him— for what he did to me that night, not so far from the very spot he's standing in now in his own puddle of piss—but there's a part of me who understands karma. You're the worst kind, packing him in that hot trunk with a rotting body. This is all you. He's suffered just about enough, and I have no interest in intercepting.

"Wait!" he says again, holding out his hands, and he's taken a wide stance, and I laugh because it looks like a comedy show. I can't be sure if it's the fact that he's wet himself, or his ugly brown uniform, or the look of terror in his eyes that make it so amusing. What he says next gets my attention, and it isn't funny.

"I know who sent the letters."

"What letters?" you ask, cocking your head to the side. He has your attention too, and you shouldn't be so quick to give yourself away.

He tries to speak, to say more, but he stutters.

"Those letters you've been getting... I know who sent them..."

You shift. "Who?" you say and you furrow your brow.

"What do you say we make a deal?" he says, but his voice shakes and he should know better. People who make deals appreciate a bit of confidence, and he has none. "You know him. He lives in your neighborhood... he's the one who messed you up with the baby...says he knows your ex-girlfriend or something..."

"You're full of shit," you tell him. But even I can see you're not so sure.

I study your expression, wondering how you're going to respond, and I'm about to go over to the motherfucker and get the information in my own way, but I force myself to stand back, giving you the chance. You're thinking, working on your next move, I can see it on your face. And just when I think you're about to speak, you fire the gun, hitting him in the face. It's gruesome the way parts of his head splatter, the way he falls to the ground, landing in the puddle of piss. What a way to die.

"Oh shit," you say, and you bite down on your bottom lip. You look over at me. "I didn't mean to do that."

My jaw twitches involuntary and fuck. I shrug. "But you did."

~

CHAPTER SEVENTEEN

KATE

I bury my face in my hands and I rub hard at my eyes, trying to figure out where to go from here. The cop is laying on the ground, his face shot to pieces, and now we have two corpses and a mystery on our hands, and all you can say is how this is all my fault. It takes two to tango, you know, but you'll never hear it. As we prepare the bodies for burial, I mentally run down the list of all the people we know who could have sent those notes. The bad part is, whoever it is, it means they know about us. It means they're on to who and what we are. It means they've been watching us—they could be watching us now.

"Something has to change, Kate," you say, catching me off guard. I look up and watch you piling rocks into the body bag.

"And by something, you mean me…"

You look up, and I'm surprised to see that it isn't anger I see in your expression, it isn't sadness. It's indifference. And this is how I know it's worse than I thought.

∼

I PULL IN THE DRIVE AFTER YOU, AND I WATCH YOU SITTING IN your car. You don't shut off the ignition, and you don't make a move to go inside. I pull in the garage after you, and I wait, but when you still don't get out of the car, I open the passenger door and climb in beside you. For several minutes we sit in silence, until the ringing in my ears lets me know I can't take it anymore. "Who do you think it is?" I ask. It takes me a bit to work up the courage, and in doing so I have to swallow my pride. I don't want to talk to you, and yet I do. I need to know what you're thinking. I need the silence to dissipate. I need answers.

You sigh. "I think that cop was full of shit..."

I cock my head and look at you straight on. "Come on, Jude. How would he have known about those notes?"

You stare straight ahead. "Maybe it was him sending them."

"Maybe," I say. "But I don't think so."

You don't say anything, but you white knuckle the steering wheel and I hate it when you won't fight back.

"What are we going to do?"

"We? What are WE going to do? Why don't you tell me, Kate? You're the one who just fucking killed a cop."

I scoff. Your tone is a bit bitter for my taste, and there's nothing worse. "You know as well as I do that so long as there's no body, there's no crime."

You look over at me and there's no light in your eyes. "Make no mistake. They'll look. Extensively. You'd just better pray they come up empty-handed."

"Then we have to go," I tell you. "We have to leave..."

I watch your jaw tighten. "You know, Kate, maybe it's you who has to go," you say. You won't look at me and you are a master at dishing out pain without even lifting a finger.

◦∼

WE'VE ARRIVED HOME AFTER OLIVIA, AND I WATCH THE TWO of you together as she excitedly tells you about what a great first day of school she had. It's just one more reason for you to be irritated, because you weren't here for her, even though I'm fairly certain you just want something else to be annoyed at me about. This is a new low for us, that's for sure. If you ask me, and you haven't, I think we need to have sex and put this whole thing to bed for good.

In the meantime, tonight just happens to be Bunko night, and I have some neighbors to visit with. If I have to do this the old fashioned way using process of elimination, then so be it. As luck would have it, Sarah is hosting tonight, and even though she and her husband are the people I'd suspect the least, Sarah knows everyone's business and she's a people pleaser to the core, and this makes her ideal to begin with.

~

WITH THE EXCEPTION OF WHO WENT ON VACATION WHEN, Sarah isn't giving me much to go on. These details make it easy to eliminate who our guy is based upon his or her whereabouts at the time the notes were sent. Unfortunately, I come up mostly empty-handed, as anyone even remotely interesting or suspect appears to have been at the wedding when the first note arrived. That makes everyone a suspect. Also, it could be that we don't know the sender at all.

I'm in the process of grilling Sarah on the people who live in our neighborhood, which I haven't met yet.

"You know anyone dark and mysterious?" I ask. "Anyone worth gossiping about?"

"Well, aren't you inquisitive tonight?" she says, eyeing me over her wine glass.

"It happens when I drink," I reply, which is a lie because I've only been pretending to drink for solidarity.

She considers me carefully and I can see that she's more suspicious than she wants to let on. Thankfully my phone rings and saves the day.

I glance down at it and see the nanny's name light up the screen. I shrug letting her know I need to take it.

"Excuse me," I offer and she smiles.

"Sophia?" I say placing it to my ear.

"Miss Kate?"

"Yes."

I hear her hesitation. "I was just wondering…"

She's holding back, and it's irritating. "Wondering what?" I ask, a hard edge to my voice.

"Well, it's just that I wished you would have told me…"

"Told you what?" I ask, and my tone lets her know she needs to get on with it.

"I just really need the hours…"

"Sophia, for God's sake—SPIT IT OUT. What are you talking about?"

"You didn't tell me you guys were going on a trip."

I shake my head, even though she obviously can't see me. "What do you mean?"

"I saw Mr. Jude packing the kids' things…"

I furrow my brow. "You saw him packing?"

"Yeah, I watched him on the baby monitor. I didn't want to say anything…but…I need this job. I was counting on the hours and…well…"

I don't wait for her to finish her thought. "You'll have your hours," I tell her, and I hit the button to end the call. I'm out the door before it hangs up.

~

"You're home early," you say, and I can tell by your tone and your body language that either your anger has subsided, or you're playing me, and given what the nanny told me I'm going with the latter.

"Yeah, I'm beat," I reply, looking around for suitcases. I don't see any.

I inhale and let it out slowly. You're sitting at your laptop, staring at the screen, and you still haven't met my eye. "Say... the Powells invited us for dinner next week. I told them I'd check with you..."

"I'm game if you are," you tell me, looking up but not really looking at me, confirming my suspicion. You are one fine liar, you are.

"You're sure you'll be in town?"

"So far as I know," you reply, and you purse your lips.

"Those letters," I say, going a different direction, giving the lump in my throat time to subside. "We need to talk about them..."

"What about them?"

I need to know if you're planning to leave because of them, or because of me. It's pretty obvious given the circumstances and your lying, but I need to be sure. If for no other reason than it's nice to see the knife coming before one stabs you in the back with it. "Have you given any thought to who it might be?"

"No."

"We can't just ignore the obvious," I say.

"I don't think we have anything to worry about," you reply, and I've lost track of your lies.

"We have everything to worry about."

"Look, Kate," you say, and it's the first time in this conversation you actually appear genuine. "Whoever is messing with us is doing just that. If they wanted to harm us, they would've already done so."

"Huh," I say, letting you believe I'm actually considering this absurdity. "Well, I've given it some thought...it's one reason I came home actually," I add and you study me intently. "I think maybe you're right. I think maybe it's time we move."

You abandon your laptop; you stand and walk toward me. When you're standing opposite me you stop and smile, although barely, and it's supposed to be a peace offering, a treaty of sorts, but I see it for what it is. A lie. You place your hands on my waist, and I let you pull me in close. "We're fine right where we are," you promise. I bury my face into your neck, my head in the sand. "How about a trip then? We could just get away for a while," I suggest, giving you the benefit of the doubt, hoping against the odds.

"You worry too much," you tell me. You rub my back, placating me, and you know I hate it when you do that.

"So I take it that's a no?" I say, and it's a shot in the dark, but I offer it anyway.

"That's a no," you reply, and I hold my breath until the dizziness comes. Because if I know anything about people, it's if they have one foot out the door, inevitably they leave.

~

CHAPTER EIGHTEEN

JUDE

I'm up and out the door early. The sun is just coming over the horizon, and it feels like not only a new day, but also the chance for a fresh start. Speaking of starts, I've decided, on a whim, to take up running. You weren't up when I left, but I wasn't sure what else to do, and this whole running thing seemed the best idea I could come up with until it isn't. I'm certainly not out of shape to begin with, but I wasn't prepared for this. My feet hit the pavement, my head whirls, and I can hear blood thrumming in my ears. I keep going because what else can I do? I need to think, and I can't think in that house, not around you.

It feels absolutely ball-busting that I've let things get this far. There are so many things I want to say to you, and so many things I can't. I packed some of the kids' things yesterday, just in case. Maybe I should start with that. A part of me wants to, out of spite, but I know I have to keep my cards tucked close to my heart.

I saw it in you last night after the situation with the cop—you're planning on running, and I wonder what would happen if I beat you to it. You can't keep running away, Kate.

There comes a time when you have to stay and deal with things like an adult. A concept which seems to have missed you all together.

I suspect that you know I'm up to something, and maybe you already realize this about me, or maybe not, but I am not the kind of man who sticks it out, who stays through thick and thin. Some days with you it feels like trying to squeeze a hurricane into a bottle. And I understand now more than I ever have before. In the end, Mother Nature always wins.

You have to pick yourself up and keep going. You have to cut your losses. Eventually you've got to let go, let nature and people do what they do.

Only, with you though, nothing is that simple. Which is how I know this is about as bad as it gets. You have to die. You can't keep someone from running forever. You can't lock a person up forever, can you? Eventually, they'll find their way out, eventually they'll go. And I can't let you take my kids or my heart with you when you go. You will not win this fight, Kate. Not because you can't. But because I won't let you. You want to go to war, fine. But war is ugly and dirty and lots of people die.

～

IT TAKES ABOUT TWO MILES BEFORE I FINALLY HIT MY STRIDE. It could be that it simply has to do with my proximity to you. The further away I get from that house, from our problems, the better I feel. There's lightness in my step, and I can finally breathe again. I consider my options, left or right, this way or that, and I can't help but think that's all life is, a series of choices we make, each one leading to the next.

I round the corner and nearly collide with an elderly couple, and I wonder how they've made it this far. They didn't give up. They haven't killed each other yet, and is it bad to want to be more like that? She steps out of the way, allowing her husband to pass first, and I wonder if they've ever come this close to doing what I think I have to do. It's impossible to be married for any length of time and not have plotted your spouse's death at least once. Love is dynamic that way. It's not supposed to be easy. I know that. I'm not interested in easy anyway. I don't want a submissive partner. I don't want a woman who steps to the side. I want a woman who knows what she wants— a woman who refuses to submit willingly—and apparently that's exactly what I got. You aren't going to step aside Kate, but you aren't going to stop running either. I know that about you. Which confirms it. You have to die.

I STOP IN THE PARK AND WATCH A WOMAN WALKING HER DOGS. She's complaining to someone on the phone, not to mention completely unaware of her surroundings, and for a moment I almost feel something. I don't like it. You would never be that stupid, but now is not the time to count my blessings. I sit there for a long while staring at people, not really seeing them, and yet, at the same time really seeing them. It's funny how much you can see when you stop looking. I know that doesn't make sense, but right now nothing does.

I don't like this feeling, this recklessness. That's always been you, and I guess you're finally rubbing off on me. I'm not the kind of man who loses control. I'm not the kind of man who loses anything. But in this case, I have two children to protect, which is the main reason I know I can't just let you go. Of course, you will try. You are a runner. It's what you've always done. Which is too bad. I really don't want you to have to die.

IT ISN'T EASY TO KILL A PERSON YOU LOVE. I KNOW. I'VE BEEN there, done that. Still, I can't help but wonder what it will be like, the last time I see you. I don't remember what the last time feels like, not even with my mother. For the life of me, I can't remember if she was sad or happy or hurried or relieved, even in those final moments before she and my father drove away. I think that's the funny thing about last times, they're selfish that way. They don't leave you, they don't let go. Especially not when only one of you is in on the fact that it's actually goodbye.

Amy didn't know it was the last time, and neither did I, not really. But you are different, and if I know you, you'll know. I want the chance to say my piece, I want the chance to make love one last time. I want to share a glass of wine and a funny joke and all the things normal couples take for granted. But we're not normal. Hell, we're not even really happy, and so there comes a time when one has a decision to make. You've gotten reckless in your killing. You say the voices are coming back, and if I didn't know better I'd say you no longer give a fuck. So, to me, it seems the time has come. You've killed so many people, Kate. Some justified, some not, and I know what you'll say, who gets to decide?

And yet, our ship is sinking, and you stopped doing your part to keep it afloat. Worse yet, now you're poking holes in the bottom. What am I supposed to do? What would a hypothetical captain do?

I'll tell you. He would be a leader. He would understand that there was a decision to be made. He'd know that he would either have to remove the threat or watch the whole crew go down. In this case, I am the captain, and that means making sacrifices. Sometimes that sacrifice happens to be a person. And sometimes that person is someone you love. Sometimes that person is you.

So, that settles it. I will be the captain, and I will save this ship, but not you. You can only save yourself. Some people in troubled marriages stick it out. Some go to therapy. Others call it a day. But not us. We aren't like most people. Killing is what we know. It's how we settle things. We don't waste time talking about them, we don't drag them out, and we don't quit. We eliminate the threat; we take out those that are in our way. To tell the truth, looking back now, I'm not sure how this could have gone any other way. This is who we are. It's what we do. Kill or be killed. It's what we know.

I head home, thankful I only have to stuff these feelings down, that I only have to pretend for a little longer. This run has been good for me. I'm feeling much better. It's given me time to sort things out. And as I make my way back, I give a lot of thought as to how I'll do it when the time comes. I could put a bullet in you, or I could go the chemical route. Although in the past, honestly, when I've really had it, I always imagine strangling you with my bare hands. I'd like to think I have it in me—but I'm not so sure. I don't want you to suffer, not really. But I do want you to know it's coming. I'm no coward. Also, I want the chance to say goodbye. We both deserve that much. You don't believe that though. It's why I'm in this position.

~

I DIDN'T GET THE CHANCE TO SAY GOODBYE TO THE OTHER women I loved. Not my mother and not my ex-girlfriend Amy. With you, it'll be different. It has to be.

I look back on my last moments with Amy with a certain amount of regret, and there are few things in this life I regret. That day is one of the few. I can picture it all so clearly, still.

The sun is shining and it's one of those mellow golden days you think will never end. We're standing in our spot, Amy and I.

"Don't you think you'll miss me?" she asks as she takes a few steps forward, balancing on one rock and then another.

"Miss you?" I ask playfully, pretty sure where she's going but not exactly. I study her from head to toe, taking in every tiny detail, committing it to memory as though it will be the last time I lay eyes on her. Intuition is a funny thing.

She turns and looks at me, and I can't help but notice the way the sunlight reflects off of her hair. She looks like an angel. But looks can be deceiving. "If we break up."

"I won't miss you," I tell her, and she sees right through me.

She laughs, and that laugh, it's contagious. It reminds me of my mother and there has never been anyone who reminded me of her more. "Of course you will."

I shake my head. "I don't miss people. It's not my style."

She smirks, the way a person does when they're on to you. She knows when I'm lying. She always has.

"Let me take your picture," I offer, motioning to the camera. "Just in case, you know… this way I'll have something to remember you by…"

"Fine," she says, and she hands me the camera. I watch as she poses on the rock. I make her wait for no other reason than she's terrible at it. She fidgets when she's in front of the camera, and while she puts up a good front, she's not as confident as she wants the world to believe. I snap her picture using the camera I gave her for her birthday. I remember her face as she unwrapped it, back when I thought we'd be together forever.

I take a few photos, and when she's had enough she walks over to where I'm standing.

"It's just that I don't know Jude...I can't be with someone who does what you do."

"Then don't," I say, because I don't want to ruin our day, and we've been over this a million times. She wants me to change, and she can't comprehend that I can't. What she doesn't realize is that if I wanted to change, I'd do it for myself. More so, I love her. Or at least I think I do. If I could change, I would change to hold on to this feeling, to us. But this is who I am. I can't stop. It's what feeds me. Without it, I'd starve. She thinks it's a choice, but if it is, it's like choosing food or water. It's impossible to live without both and that's our problem.

"What if you got help?"

"Help. That's funny."

"Therapists can't tell on you when you confide in them, it's the law."

"I'm not seeing a shrink."

"But they could help you, Jude," she swears, and her voice grows louder, and she's getting to that point. I know it well, how irrational she can be when she reaches her point of no return. It won't be the first time she's pulled this card, and if something doesn't change, it won't be the last. She likes to take me right to the edge. She makes threats, and then when I don't agree she gives me the silent treatment and takes up with her ex. I'm not threatened by it though. I've seen the guy, from afar. I refuse to go there, to get too close, for fear that I might hurt an innocent bystander, an irrelevant player in Amy's sick little game. If he were what she wanted, she wouldn't come running back to me.

"What if I told someone," she asks, crossing her arms. "Then would you stop?"

I take a deep breath in, and I hold it. Amy likes to test me, and I refuse to let her win. But she did win, in many respects, that's why we're having this conversation. I didn't tell her that I kill people on occasion. I didn't offer that bit of information up willingly. She followed me, and she saw for herself. Worse, she saw my father, and I know if I go down, he goes down with me. Amy is one of the crazy ones that way. She constantly accused me of seeing someone else whenever my dad and I took one of our trips, and eventually I ran out of excuses. I didn't tell her the truth. I didn't have to. She found out the hard way.

"You're not going to tell anyone, Amy."

"Maybe, I'll tell my new boyfriend. Maybe— I already have…"

She likes to do this thing where she teases me and usually I ignore her. This time, I try to reason. Which turns out to be a mistake. "You haven't."

"I have," she says. "And I told him we are going to run away together. So he's out of the picture for good."

"We aren't running away."

"Why not? Maybe you need a change."

"I don't run."

"Fine." She throws up her hands. "But—if you don't promise you'll stop, then I will. I'll go, and you'll never see me again."

"You always say that."

"This time I mean it."

I shrug, because what else can I do.

"But before I go, I'll make sure to share your little secret."

I take a step toward her, and she smiles. She actually smiles. She is so sure of herself, so sure she knows me well enough to win—so sure of her place in the world, so sure love is enough.

In the end, it isn't. She didn't get to be the one who left. It turns out she didn't know me at all.

~

CHAPTER NINETEEN

KATE

I wake with a start, clutching my chest, defensively. My stomach turns, and I sit up, thinking I might be sick. I survey the room, in search of something to vomit into. Instinctively, I feel for my neck, and then I shake my head, reflexively trying my best to shake off the dream. But even more so, trying to rid myself of the images in my mind. It doesn't work, and there are dozens of them, flashes of images. Your hands around my neck, your expression as you hold me under water. The sky is moonless tonight, making our bedroom pitch black, which only makes it more difficult to see. I can't breathe, and I need help. I've been here before —it always feels the same—but never any easier. It might as well be the first time this has happened, because in times like these there's zero sense of control. I just have to ride it out, no matter what.

I imagine myself choking to death—not on water, as was the case in my dream, but on my own vomit, and this is not how I plan to die. I pat the bed in search of you until eventually, my hand settles on something warm. I can't see you in the dark, but I listen for the steady hum of your light snore, and it soothes me enough to make the bile in my throat recede. When it finally does, I inhale deeply, trying to force air into my lungs. I sit there for a bit, thinking of the dream and the look in your eyes as you held me under, as you squeezed the life out of me. I don't think I've ever seen that look before, but then I must have, if I dreamt it. When my breathing settles, I climb out of bed and make my way into the bathroom. It's still there, where I left it, the note I wrote apologizing—even though I'm really not all that sorry. Sometimes it's best to make peace. And sometimes it's best to beat people at their own game.

I MAKE MY WAY BACK TO BED, AND I LAY THERE FOR A WHILE running down the checklist of things I have to do, until I eventually realize sleep isn't likely to return. You have a meeting later this morning, I checked your phone, and as soon as you leave I plan to take the kids and go. You'll try to find us, and maybe you will, but then, maybe you won't. I consider our new life, away from here, and what leaving will mean for all of us, and I want to feel sad but instead I'm numb. I roll over and check my phone. There's still a good three hours before you and the sun are up, and so I decide to head downstairs in hopes that coffee will make me feel something. Roscoe follows, and I remember a time when I hated this dog. I can't take him with us, and that will kill the kids, but he's your dog and I'll have enough on my plate. I pause and pat his head and when he looks up at me with those curious eyes of his, I find it surprising how much he's grown on me. As the coffee brews, I pace and I wait. My stomach churns, and my heart races. I sit at the table, but my hands are shaking, and I can't stop fiddling with things. I pick up my empty mug, and I notice it shakes as I hold it in my hands. I place the cup down, watch the tremor in my fingers, and then stuff them between my thighs. When the coffee is ready, I stand, walk over to the counter and fill my mug. Roscoe sits at my feet, staring up at me as though to say 'what now.'

"I don't know," I say to him and no one, and I cup the mug with my hands, the heat burning into me, but at least I feel something. I don't know how long I stood there that way, staring into nothingness, but one thing is for sure, I'll never forget the scream that jarred me out of it.

~

RACING TO THE FRONT DOOR, I STOP ONLY TO SLIP ON FLIP-flops, and then I hurriedly punch in the alarm code into the keypad, fling open the door and step out on to the porch. I look back over my shoulder, and then I shut the door slowly behind me. Before it closes all the way, Roscoe cocks his head to the side, clearly confused. I stand there for a moment, he's scratching at the door, and I know if I don't open it, he'll wake you or the kids. He senses something is wrong, and he won't stop scratching, wanting to be let out. The last thing I need is you coming down, insisting I'm crazy, so I open the door. He waits for my command because that's what he's been trained to do, and then he steps out and he sits at my side.

I reach down and pat his head. "Show me where it came from," I tell him and in no time flat, he does.

~

THE DOG DARTS ACROSS THE STREET. I LAG NOT FAR BEHIND. It's muggy out, and everything is still. All cylinders are firing, and I know this feeling. It's instinctive; I know when something is wrong. If you pay enough attention, you can sense evil, deep down in your bones. Maybe it's a law of attraction thing, I don't know. But I half-walk, half-run to keep up with Roscoe. I follow him almost the entire length of our street until we're stopped in front of the Morris'. Anne's house. It doesn't seem possible that I could have heard a scream this far, but I make a mental note to ask you about the distance sound travels. You would know such things.

Roscoe stops suddenly, as though he isn't sure. I hold up my hand, a signal I learned from you, telling him to halt. He sits at my side and watches the house, panting relentlessly while I contemplate my next move. I glance down at him, as though suddenly he might tell me what I need to know. He improvises by not taking his gaze away from the front door. Even from where I'm standing I can see that there's a light on somewhere in the house, possibly several lights. I suspect it's coming from the rear of the house, which makes it plausible that Roscoe is right, and this is indeed where the scream came from. I stand there for a moment longer, wondering if I should just walk up to the door or simply go home, when I'm fairly certain I see a light turn off and then back on, and I decide it won't hurt to get a better look. I walk around to the side of the house, and I'm disappointed when I try the latch on the back fence and find it's locked from the inside. This is going to be more work than I thought. It isn't until I'm climbing the gate, hurling myself over the fence, that I wish I'd finished my coffee. It's been awhile since I've climbed fences. To make matters worse, just as I've managed to get one leg over, a floodlight comes on, halting all thought, clearing my head. I throw the other leg over and I drop suddenly, just in case anyone's looking. Only I hit the ground harder than I expect, and I lie there for a moment, waiting for the pain to come. When it doesn't, and when the light finally goes off, I pull myself up. I hobble over to the gate and open it for Roscoe. I didn't think to bring a weapon, and he's the best I've got, only he's panting hard and I can tell he's agitated.

"Quiet, boy," I hiss, and instantly I realize bringing the dog was a mistake. He's an animal. Of course, he isn't going to stay quiet when he perceives a threat.

I command him to stay, and then I order him back out of the gate, hoping I'm using the proper hand signal. I'm actually surprised when he goes but I wait for a second making sure he's not going to give me away by barking or scratching at the fence and when it seems the coast is clear, I slowly walk around to the back-side of the house. I perch down behind the patio furniture and peer in through the large glass window, which offers a decent view of both the kitchen and the dining room. There are lights on but I don't see any movement inside, just empty rooms. I wait and I wait and I wait until I have to pee and I'm just about ready to give up. I can hear someone speaking inside although I can't make out what is being said. From out here, it sounds like garbled background noise, and for all I know it could be a TV. I'm doing the pee dance wondering what I was thinking, and I'm just about to turn to go when something gray catches my eye. When I lean in closer, I see Anne's husband come around the corner. He enters the kitchen and I watch as he takes a glass tumbler and hurls it into the sink. He stands there for a moment, both hands resting on the counter top, head hanging down. Then he turns slowly and unexpectedly toward the back door and he looks out into the darkness and straight at me. I flinch involuntarily, even though I'm fairly certain that despite the fact that I can see him, he can't see me. Even so, there's something in his expression that is dark and evil, something I haven't seen before, something I recognize. "Get Sophia," he calls backward over his shoulder, and then he turns and pulls a glass from the shelf and pours himself a glass of whiskey. *Gentleman Jack*, I'd know that label anywhere. It was my father's drink of choice. He kicks back the contents of the glass and pours himself another.

There's something curious and a bit sinister in his expression and in what he does next. I find it peculiar the way he reaches down and lifts broken glass; he places it at eye level and he studies it. Eventually, he returns it to the counter top and then he stands up straight and he loosens his collar. He pulls a cigarette from his shirt pocket and lights it on the stove. Then he shifts and leans forward to open the window over the sink. He's staring out into the dark again, deep in thought, milking that cigarette for all it's worth, as though it's his last.

Eventually, Anne walks into the dining room. Sophia trails not far behind. She's wearing some weird nightgown thing, and I feel silly for not having realized she lived here all along. It bothers me, though I'm not sure why I'd never thought to ask.

"Sit down," Anne tells her, and she does as she's told. She places her hands in her lap, and she picks at her nails. But her eyes, they never leave Anne. There's a bit of hesitation in her demeanor, which isn't surprising seeing that it's not quite yet four in the morning.

"What did I tell you?" I hear Stanley ask, although I'm not sure to whom he's speaking because he's still staring out the window, straight at me. For a moment, I convince myself that maybe he actually sees me. He takes a long pull on the cigarette and exhales out the kitchen window, pushing smoke into the night air, and then he shifts toward the dining room.

"I know. I'm sorry…" Sophia says, and she stares at Anne.

Anne walks over to her husband and takes the cigarette from his mouth. "What did I tell you about smoking?" she asks and she eyes him intently but I can't discern whether it's a look of contempt or not. When he doesn't answer she turns and walks back over to where Sophia is sitting in the chair. She reaches down and presses the cigarette to Sophia's forearm, essentially putting out the flame. Even from where I'm standing I can see tears well up in Sophia's eyes but she doesn't flinch and she doesn't make a sound.

"Well, at least this one doesn't scream..." Stanley sighs, and it draws my attention back to him. He's removing his belt, and then he rolls up his sleeves. He walks over to his wife and addresses Sophia. "But you've always been a good girl, haven't you? The kind who handles pain as though you know what to do with it. You tuck it away like it's nothing. I know a thing or two about that, don't I? That kind of pain— it feels a lot like the pain of being cheated..." He pauses just long enough to take a breath and then he slowly shakes his head. "DON'T I?"

She's holding his gaze, and I can't look away. "Yes, sir," she says obediently, but there's defiance in her stare.

Anne speaks as he wraps the belt around Sophia's neck, and this is when I know I have to go in. I told Sophia I'd give her those hours, and in that moment I decide not to be a liar.

"Because of you, I had to send the kids to my mother-in-law's..." Anne whines. "And you know how much I hate doing that, don't you? Surely, you can remember the last time?"

"Yes," Sophia says.

Anne scoffs. "Tell me then, why do you all insist on misbehaving?"

"I...I—" Sophia starts to reply, but I can't see what is happening because I have to get in that house and soon.

I crouch down, making my way toward the window, listening as Stanley interrupts his wife. Unlike her, he speaks low, steady and calm. Like a natural. "How many times have I told you… it's your responsibility to make sure those girls bring me my money…"

"She meant to, she did… the family… they're just late paying her…" she tells him, and she is smart. She doesn't make promises, not the way most people in her situation would, and I like that about her.

He exhales. I don't have a visual but I hear every breath, every word. "I don't want to hear your excuses. What do you think I keep you girls around for?" he yells. "My health? No! You're here to make me money, and that's that. And when you fail to do so… when you fail to hold up your end of the bargain…well…I hate it. I really hate it."

"Come on, darling," Anne says just as I'm about through the window. It feels good to have a visual again, only I have no plan, and if they see me, they see me. Thankfully, as usual they're only focused on themselves. "You know you like it just a little. How else are we supposed to stay entertained around here? In this suburban hell-hole…"

"You have a point," Stanley agrees.

Anne folds her lips, although her expression seems less than disappointed. "It's just… I've told you and I've told you and I've told you…you're not allowed to kill them."

"I know," he says and I watch his demeanor change.

"Now, be a good little boy and get on your knees. Let Sophia see you beg mommy for forgiveness."

I watch as he does as she orders, and I'm perched on their kitchen counter like some fucking comic book character trying to find a way to hop down without drawing attention to myself, and what the fuck is happening here? I should be thinking about how I'm going to pull this off, seeing as I haven't brought a weapon. I should be thinking about how to not get myself killed. Instead, all I can think about is how I can't wait to tell you about this.

~

WHILE STANLEY BOY IS ON HIS KNEES, I MANAGE TO CLIMB down off the counter and quietly tiptoe through the short hallway into the Morris' office. I have to squint my eyes to see, but when I get to the doorway I'm happy to see a table lamp has been left on. I have to flatten myself as much as possible as I squeeze inside the door, in hopes that I won't be seen from the dining room. Even with the table lamp on, the room is dark, which is likely due to the fact that it's a wood paneled room, dark oak, with wall-to-wall bookshelves and a large mahogany desk in the center. I make my way over to the desk. I survey the contents on top and then I carefully open the top drawer. Rummaging around, I find a letter opener, which could do for a weapon if nothing else. Almost satisfied, I'm just about to close the drawer, to move onto the next drawer, when something familiar catches my eye. It's a box of notecards. Familiar-looking note cards. I reach for the box, lifting the lid and pulling one out. I turn it over in my hands, feeling the weight of the paper. *Of course.* They just so happen to be the same notecards the letters were sent on. Now that I have even more inspiration, aside from hearing Sophia pleading, I move on. It isn't until I reach the third drawer that I find the small safe; the kind I know isn't used for anything aside from cash or handguns. The only problem is it has a punch pad, and I don't know the code. I try their street address. No luck. *Come on, don't fail me now.* Frustrated, I try their son's birthday. No luck. Their anniversary. It has to be their anniversary. The only trouble is, I don't remember when that is. I move the mouse on the computer praying it's not password-protected. Of course it is. I try the first two combinations. When I type in their street address, suddenly I'm in. I pull up the calendar, and Sophia is crying, and goddamn it, this is taking too long. I could just as easily have walked back into the kitchen and grabbed a knife. Sure, they would've heard me, but perhaps the element of surprise would have been in my favor. I type the word 'anniversary' and eventually theirs pops up. Thank God, they're the kind of people who put their own anniversary on the calendar. But then, of course, they are.

I punch the numbers into the safe. It pops open. But it also chimes, and I know without a doubt that kind of sound didn't go unnoticed. I know because I hear the footsteps making their way toward me, and they're too heavy to be anyone's other than Stanley's.

I PRACTICALLY DIVE UNDER THE DESK AND STEADY MY breathing. I smell him before I see him. He reeks of expensive cologne, stale cigarettes, and old whiskey. He stops when he's about three feet from the desk and I know what he's staring at, the open drawer. From his vantage point, I'm pretty certain he can't see the safe, and what's missing, and this is why I gather he comes closer to get a better look. I wait for him to get as close as possible. I grip the letter opener, running my finger around its smooth, sharp edge, hoping it'll be enough to do the trick. When he takes one more step forward, I lean forward with everything I've got and use the blade to slice through his Achilles tendon. It's a good thing the Morrises like expensive things; it's probably the best letter opener on the market. I can tell by the way he screams and drops to the floor.

All of a sudden, we're eye to eye, and I like that I get to watch as the realization hits his face. He says my name. I reach forward, aiming for his neck, but he pulls back quickly, and I slice through his right cheek instead. His hand flies to his face; blood pours from between his fingers. I watch as it drips down his arm and out onto the oak floor, but not for long. He only gives me a second to jump up and ready the gun.

"It's not loaded," he says, and I decide to call his bluff and aim for his knee. He flinches, and I know he's lying. He holds up his hands. "Okay."

"What in God's name," Anne interrupts as she leans in the doorway.

"Kate?"

Stanley has pretty much managed to back into the corner and he is crouched down as though he and the wall might become one.

"Sit," I order, taking aim at Anne. I point to the office chair and watch as she does as I say.

When I have her attention, I decide I want answers. "Why did you send those notes?"

"Oh, those," she says as if it were nothing. "We just wanted to be friends… we wanted to play too."

I purse my lips. "No you didn't."

"Amy was my girlfriend," Stanley says.

"Amy?" I ask, cocking my head.

"Yes, Amy. And your husband, he took her away."

"I told Stanley to let it go," Anne interrupts again and her tone is biting. "But he just couldn't let it go…it was all he could talk about…the way your Jude stole her from him."

"It was," he chides. "It was his fault she went missing. It was too much for her. She was never a cheater."

"I beg to differ," I tell him.

"Me too," Anne agrees.

"It was you," I say suddenly clearer than ever. "You attacked me."

Stanley shakes his head. But he's lying.

"Stanley say goodbye to your wife."

"Please, Kate…it wasn't me. You saw the guy, they arrested him…"

I walk to Anne until I'm standing over her. I place the gun to her right temple. Point blank range. She doesn't say anything else, which I find surprising. "I'm going to give you one chance to save yourself…Did your husband have anything to do with me losing my child?"

She nods, and tears stream down her face. "I told him to let it go. But he never could. He had to get even…I told him. I just wanted you guys to move… so he'd let this whole ex-girlfriend thing go," she tells me, and I almost feel sorry for her. I know about girls like Amy and the havoc they can wreak.

"Thanks," I say, and then I fire. Stanley sobs and he covers his face. I look up to see Sophia standing in the doorway, covered in clumps of brain and bone and blood. Also, pieces of Anne's hair. She's wide-eyed, but there's something interesting in her expression. I swear she's almost smiling. I point the gun in Stanley's direction, and then I drop my hand and look over at Sophia.

"Do you want to do it?" I ask and I watch her face as she considers my question.

She shrugs slightly. "I don't know how to shoot…"

"Oh, it's easy."

Stanley cries.

"You just point in the direction you want the bullet to go and squeeze the trigger."

She juts out her bottom lip. "Okay, then."

I hand her the gun, and her hands shake. Stanley prays. He pleads with her. He says he's sorry. For everything. Tears stream down his face, and mix with blood. I wonder if the salt in them stings the gaping hole in his cheek, and I hope so. Sophia repositions herself and takes aim.

I don't think she'll do it.

But she does.

When he slumps forward, she places the gun on the desk.

I eye her. "I thought you said you didn't know how to shoot."

"I only shoot animals."

I smile. "That makes sense."

～

IT'S LIKELY THE COPS ARE ALREADY ON THEIR WAY, I TELL Sophia hurriedly. I lift a handkerchief from the desk and use it to wipe the gun. Then using the handkerchief to aid me, I place Anne's fingers around it and I position the gun in her hands. Her face is mostly gone, and the weapon looks almost comedic resting on her thigh.

I check the time on my phone. "In exactly, two minutes, you're going to call 911. I want you to tell them that you were sleeping when you heard gunshots. Can you sound sleepy? Give me your best sleepy voice…"

"Hello," she offers and it's better than I expected.

"Now— tell them you heard gunshots and that you're afraid and then hang up. They'll call back. Do NOT answer."

She nods and I pause making sure she understands. "Then," I say. "When they get here, make sure the front door is open. I want you to sit in the hall just outside and pretend to be in shock…"

She nods again. "Do you know what shock means?"

She shakes her head from side to side. "It means you don't speak at all. If you have to, repeat the same words over and over. When they ask, which they'll do a lot, tell them you don't know what happened in here, in this office…Tell them you found Anne lying in a pool of blood and that you tried to help…"

She looks up at me. "So I don't tell them about you?"

"No. Never."

She narrows her eyes. "Can I still come to work?"

"Of course. They'll want to interview you and they'll ask you a lot of questions. Questions about your injuries and how the Morrises treated you… act like you're in shock."

She nods slowly.

"Promise me," I say.

She does.

"Miss Kate," she calls after me as I turn to go. I lift my leg to step over the mess and then I stop and meet her eye.

"Yes?"

"What about the others?"

I cock my head. "The others?"

"The girls in the attic…"

I look up. "Girls?" I ask and as the words roll off my tongue, it suddenly clicks.

"How many are there?"

"Eight. Or…nine…counting me."

I take a deep breath and exhale considering what to say.

"Do you think they know I'm here?"

She shakes her head.

"Then tell the police the truth. About everything. Everything but about who shot who. Tell them you were asleep, and whatever you do…don't tell them about me."

She glances at the floor and then at Anne.

"Do you understand, Sophia?"

She looks up slowly. When she meets my eye I can see that she does.

～

CHAPTER TWENTY

JUDE

"Why do we have to go?" Olivia whines. "Mom promised she was gonna make pancakes," she tells me, rubbing at her sleepy eyes.

I peer at her in the rearview mirror. "You're just going to stay with Grandpa for a few hours, so Daddy can run some errands— and then we'll have pancakes…for lunch."

"Are you and Mom fighting again?" Brady asks.

"Your mom and I—we don't fight."

"Right," he says, and I swear, he's four going on thirty.

I focus on the road, at the task at hand, and I don't know how I'll raise them without you, I really don't. Brady with his 'special needs' and Olivia being well… a girl.

Girls need their mothers. Even I know that. But then, so do boys, and mine was pretty messed up, so there is that.

❧

MY FATHER MEETS ME AT HIS DOOR, LIKE ALWAYS, BUT HIS FACE is pale. He eyes the children and ushers them inside.

I narrow my gaze.

"I just heard on the scanner your neighborhood is swarming with cops. Something about a murder-suicide…"

"Huh," I say, playing it off, the way I always do when I suspect that anything has to do with you.

"Where's that wife of yours?"

"She went for a run."

He shakes his head. "Sure she did."

"Am I missing something?"

"Sit down, son. There's something I need to tell you."

I check my watch, more instinctively than anything else. "I'm not sure I have time."

"Make time," he says, and he steps out onto the porch, shutting the door behind him. He looks me in the eye, and he waits. I don't sit, and when he figures out I'm not going to, he gets on with it. "Did you kill her?"

"What?" I ask, and I wasn't sure what he was going to tell me, but I can say for sure I didn't expect him to lead with that.

"Your wife. Did you kill her?"

I do a double-take, as though what he's just suggested is the most absurd thing in the world, the farthest thought in my mind. "Of course not."

He studies me for a moment, and then he inhales and lets it out slowly. "There's something I've been meaning to tell you, for a long time, Jude," he says and he rubs at his jawline, making it clear that this conversation isn't easy for him. "I know this is going to change everything. And I mean everything."

"Okay," I say, unable to come up with anything else that makes sense.

"It's just, I'd hate to see you make the same mistake I did," he tells me, and I know exactly what he means when most normal people would have doubt. This is his way of telling me my mother didn't just run off.

"It never leaves you. Never."

I swallow hard, and I shake my head. But I don't say anything in return. I head home to you.

～

RUDY WAS RIGHT. COPS ARE SURROUNDING OUR SUBDIVISION. It takes some pleading, some lying, telling them I left my dog locked up in a crate he doesn't really have, and eventually they give me permission to trek in on foot. Just down the block, I run into Sam, the neighbor who lives down the street, the redneck one who made millions selling some kind of hunting gadget. You say he gives you the creeps. He talks a lot, and so I'm pretty thankful to find him standing at the end of his drive in his pajamas.

I hold my hand up to my forehead to shield my eyes from the sun and look in the direction of our place. "What's going on?"

"Man… you don't want to know," he says, taking a slow sip from his mug, gazing down the street. Sam is the kind of guy who almost never looks you in the eye.

I turn to him. "Actually, I do."

He looks up at me then, and he seems taken aback, as though he's put off someone would address him so directly. "Oh," he says. "Anne and Stanley… you know, the yuppies down there?" he asks pointing toward their house, which is barely visible around the corner. "Turns out, they had some messed up shit goin' on in that house."

"Like what?"

He slurps at his coffee. "Like slaves…"

"Slaves?"

"Yeah… and rumor is, they're dead in there…"

I furrow my brow. You were right. This guy is weird.

He shifts and turns his head toward me slightly, but he

keeps his gaze focused down the road. "You hear anything funny this morning?"

"Funny?" I shake my head. "No. I haven't been home…"

"I heard gunshots. Two of 'em. I know a gunshot when I hear it."

"Hmm." I say, and he looks at me then.

He juts out his bottom lip. "Which means all those slaves… they died some other kinda way."

~

"KATE!" I CALL OUT, GOING FROM ROOM TO ROOM. "KATE!" I yell once more, and I inhale and exhale loudly, annoyed by this game of hide and seek that I hadn't agreed to. I've checked all over the house, and you're nowhere to be found. Your car is in the garage, but I know you, and that means nothing.

I make my way upstairs again, and check the one place I realize I hadn't thought to look: the bathroom. I walk in and there you are, eyes closed, soaking in the tub, filled to the brim with bubbles.

"Kate," I say, and you don't open your eyes.

"Kate."

"You're back," you murmur, but you still refuse to look at me.

"What in the fuck happened at the Morrises?"

"They died."

"I heard that. How?"

You twist your lips, and you open your eyes slowly, as though you're remembering something long forgotten. You look right at me, and you shrug.

I exhale. "Damn it, Kate."

You look at me then, and I mean really look at me. You tell me what happened in that house, and I don't know how I missed it. The truth is, I missed a lot of things, you being one of them. But when you offer up the details, I don't know what to say, other than I'm impressed, but even those words can't manage to find their way out, so instead I keep them inside, tucked close to my heart.

"You told me I was crazy, about the screams... but I wasn't wrong. Those people—man, you should've heard what they were doing with those girls...some really messed-up stuff. I knew something about that woman was off. I sensed it from the get-go. I just hadn't imagined it was that bad."

I sigh, long and slow. "Yeah, I don't know how I missed it —how we all missed it—I mean, right here on our street, under our noses...it's hard to believe. Even for me. And I've seen a lot."

You cock your head and narrow your eyes. "Is everything all right?

"Well, since you asked... no. In fact, nothing is all right."

"That's what I was afraid you were going to say."

"Since when have you ever been afraid of anything?"

"Me?" you say and you do a double-take. "Oh, I'm afraid of a lot of things. I just don't like to talk about them."

I don't say anything in return. Sometimes it's best that way.

"So, let's not talk Jude. Let's just get on with what you came here to do."

I lean against the counter and cross my arms. "Which is?"

"Don't patronize me."

"I'm not."

"So you didn't come here to kill me?"

I offer a half-hearted smile. "What would make you think that?"

"We kill people. It's what we do."

"That's a fucked-up way to see the man you married."

"It's the truth…" you say, shifting in the tub. "I'd be an idiot if I didn't consider it a possibility."

"I don't want to kill you, Kate."

"And why is that?"

"I just don't."

"Well, then. What *do* you want?"

"My father just admitted he killed my mother," I tell you, and I don't mean to say it but I find myself offering it up anyway. As the words slip out, my stomach sinks. To be honest, it would be easier just to take you out, and it sure as shit would save me the trouble of explaining. And now that it's out there, it feels like I'm on one of those amusement park rides that hurl you a thousand feet into the air and I am free falling.

You sit up then, and suddenly your tits are on full display, and it makes everything instantly better. You stare at me, waiting for more, but I know better than to give it to you.

"What did you say to him?" you ask, and then you swallow hard. "Wait…and you left our kids there?"

"Rudy would never hurt the kids."

"Did you think he would kill your mother?"

"Yes, actually. I did."

~

YOU WANT TO KNOW MORE THAN I'M ABLE OR WILLING TO share, and you are relentless in your pursuit.

"Jude," you call, and it takes me a bit, but finally I have just the story to share.

I was nine, when they told me over dinner that they were taking off to Alaska for two weeks, and that they were leaving me with my father's mother. I didn't really know her, as she lived in another state. We visited once, that I could recall, for my grandfather's funeral. Pretty much the gist of what I knew about her was that she was an old woman who had my father late in life. I was aware from that brief visit that she had more money than she knew what to do with, and was paranoid as hell that anyone and everyone was out to get it.

I arrived on a Wednesday. I stood at the curb, suitcase in hand, looking up at the old country home. "You'll be fine," my mother said as she studied my expression. "You always are."

"Why do I have to stay here?" I asked, in an obvious desperate attempt of getting her to change her mind.

"Look at this place," she said. "It's the perfect opportunity for a boy like you to run around."

"Then how come dad never wants to come here?"

"Jude, darling," she said, adjusting the collar on my shirt. "Don't be so obtuse."

"What does obtuse mean?"

She gave me a look I've never forgotten. And then she smiled, "Ask your grandmother," she said. The smile was so big, it lit up her whole face, and in that moment I was happy for her, that she was going on vacation, even if it meant leaving me behind. I hadn't seen her smile like that in months.

My grandmother lived on a seventy-acre plot of land in the middle of nowhere on what had, at one time, been a profitable farm. I learned this on my first evening there when I showed up for dinner. I'll never forget the massive table she had in her dining room. It must have sat twenty, easily. I walked into the room, all washed up, that's what my father told me to do—to make sure I always washed up. The spread on the table was unimaginable to a boy like me. My mom wasn't much of a cook, and we usually had a mixture of take out and sandwiches. I could feel myself salivating at the aroma's coming off the table. Mrs. Sue, as she insisted I call her, had three cooks.

When I entered the room, she didn't look up from her paper, nor did she stop eating. She had four Bassett Hounds surrounding her, and they watched my every move. As long as I've lived, I don't think I've ever met a person who treated their animals better than they treated people on the scale that woman did, but it's probably just as well.

I cleared my throat and then I went to take the seat opposite her. She looked up at me as I pulled the chair out. "May I help you?"

I looked around the room. "Is this where I should sit?"

She cocked her head to the side. "Did that mother of yours not teach you the proper way to address a lady?"

I shrugged.

"What happened? The cat get your tongue? Don't you speak when spoken to? Or did she forget all forms of manners?"

I wasn't sure what to say, so I said nothing. Sometimes it's the best way, and sometimes it's not. That's what I learned that night.

I went to pull out a different chair.

"Not that one either," she said.

I stood and waited, thinking she was going to give me further direction, but she simply went back to eating.

"May I sit?" I finally thought to say.

"You may not."

"What am I supposed to do?"

"Well, actually it would have been nice if you'd never been born. But given it's clearly a little late for that, let me get Erma." She picked up her glass of water, took a slow sip, and swallowed, never taking her eyes from mine. "ERMA!"

Erma came running. She turned out to be the help, and

maybe the worst of them all. "Show Jude here to the stables. He shall sleep there. And make sure no one feeds him."

"Yes, Mrs. Sue."

My grandmother's eyes bore into me. "There comes a time in every boy's life where he has to learn to earn his keep. This is your time, Jude," she said. "It's such a pity that drunken mother of yours hasn't done better by you. I warned my son about her; I told him not to marry her. But that's okay. You're here now. And we all see the error of his ways."

That first week was the first time I understood what it really meant to be hungry.

～

MRS. SUE WAS RIGHT ABOUT ONE THING—IT WAS MY TIME. IT was my time for a lot of things: for learning to sleep in old barns, on dirt floors, and how if you are going to take a risk, it's best not to get caught. An old rotary telephone taught me that lesson. I was trying to call my mom, even though I had no idea how or where to reach her. It's hard to think rationally when you haven't eaten in three days. That night I decided to steal scraps from the dogs, but I didn't have much success at that either. Every night I watched as Erma fed the dogs whatever was left of the feast that Mrs. Sue had not eaten.

Erma was one of a staff of eleven which my grandmother treated only slightly better than me. And it was Erma who told Mrs. Sue about the telephone call. I remember being struck in the head with the telephone. But I don't remember much about the days following.

～

MY FEEDINGS RESUMED THREE DAYS BEFORE MY PARENTS WERE

to pick me up. I was allowed to eat as much as I wanted after the dogs had had their share, and I ate so much I made myself sick each and every time. I worked in the fields twelve hours a day doing what I was told, and I hadn't quite known pain until that summer. When you're a kid, it's hard to imagine your back aching until your knees buckle, or the tips of your fingers wearing so thin they bleed. Or sweating until you're dizzy, or the visions that come along with dehydration. It's hard to imagine and yet impossible not to, once you know the lengths humans can go to, to see others suffer.

~

I'LL NEVER UNDERSTAND WHY MY MOTHER THOUGHT IT WAS okay to leave me there, but maybe she just needed a vacation, or maybe she thought anything was survivable for two weeks. To this day I don't know, because I never saw her again.

My father, on the other hand, I understood why he left me there. It's difficult to see how bad a person is when it's your own parent, it's as though there's some sort of unbreakable bond that spans time, as though you share a connection that means if they're terrible, you must be too, and so it's best not to admit how bad it really is.

But it wasn't my parents who came to retrieve me. It was just Rudy.

"Your mother wanted a different life," he told me when I asked where she was. "And sometimes when you love a person, you have to let them have what they want."

"But I don't want her to have a different life."

He looked at me with understanding. "No one ever does, son. No one does."

I sucked in my bottom lip. "What does that mean?"

"It means that we'll probably spend the rest of the summer here with your Grandmother."

A lump formed in my throat. "I don't want to stay here."

"Touché."

"What does touché mean?"

He placed his hand on my shoulder and gave it a hard squeeze. "It means that someday you'll be older, and you'll see for yourself, and then you'll understand why people make the choices they do."

∼

I FINISH MY STORY, AND YOUR EYES ARE ON MINE. YOU SWITCH on the tap and add more bubbles.

"Come here, get in," you say. And I do.

You wrap your arms around me, and we stay that way until the water turns cold.

∼

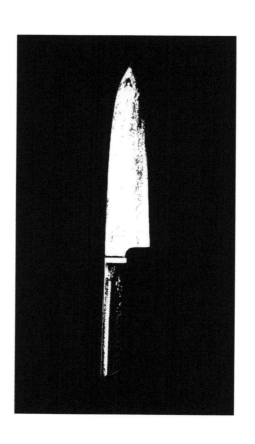

CHAPTER TWENTY-ONE

KATE

W e're finally able to get out of our neighborhood, and we're on our way to Rudy's to pick up the kids, when you change everything. Neither of us is sure where to go from here. That much is clear. Our neighborhood is swarming with cops and news crews, and neither of us wants to address what's going on. So we don't talk about it, not really. We're numbed out, hollow, empty. We're what you are when you've given your all and you're not sure what's left to give. We love each other, sure, but there's a deeper unspoken question that hangs in the air between us: Is love enough? It was back there in our bathroom and it is for now. It's clear, though, that some things bring you together and others tear you apart, and what comes next is often anyone's guess.

"I think we should go to marriage counseling," you say, looking over at me.

I study your expression, waiting for the punch line, and when it's apparent there isn't one, I shake my head slowly.

"We need this, Kate."

"You know me," I say. "I don't do therapy."

"It's just a conversation," you tell me.

I cock my head, and I can't believe these words are coming from your mouth. "Why do we need a third party to have a 'conversation?'"

You stare out the windshield for a long time without answering, and I can see that you're thinking it over. I chew on my bottom lip, and I consider for a moment that this is some sort of joke.

"I can't have you running, Kate."

"I'm right here."

"You won't stay."

I glance away and then back at you. "Say's who?"

"I know you."

I scoff. "You *think* you do."

"That's why we have an appointment with the therapist tomorrow," you say. You smile, but it's half-hearted. "To find out."

~

'House of horrors,' the headlines read. 'Terror in suburbia,' others say. 'Evil in plain sight.'

"Can you believe it?" Josie says. I've heard this before, but she's the last to call. The rest of the neighbors have all called or come around, one by one. Each of them asking the same question. *Can you believe it?*

"No," I tell her, and it's only a partial lie. But that's what bothers me. I both can and can't understand what's occurred right down the street. I'm a walking contradiction, and everything makes sense in hindsight.

"Yeah, well," she remarks. "Remember what happened at your party?"

"Yes," I say.

"Everything makes so much sense," she tells me hurriedly, and that much we can agree on. "It's like they unraveled before our eyes, you know, like a mental breakdown or something," Josie says, and she's not wrong but she's not exactly right either.

I hang up the phone and field another call. You turn on the news, and I switch it off. Details are starting to emerge about what took place in that house, and they don't add up.

Nine immigrants found dead. Human trafficking at its worst, I hear the newscaster say when you switch it back on.

"Are you sure, Kate? There's nothing tying you to this."

"We've been over and over it," I say, and I shake my head. "Like I told you. I shot Anne and Stanley and then I left. Those girls were alive, as far as I know."

"But you didn't see them alive?"

"No."

You sigh and you leave it at that. I follow suit. I don't tell you about the missing link, I don't tell you about Sophia because I know what you'll say. You'll say we need to run. That it's just a matter of time before she spills the beans to the cops, if she hasn't already.

But the thing is, I promised you I wouldn't run. The fact that we would be doing it together matters little.

I'm tired of running, Jude.

It's time to face the music, whatever that might be.

~

EVENTUALLY, I JOIN YOU IN BED, BUT I DON'T SLEEP. My heart races, and I consider that it's just a matter of time before the cops show up at our door. It's possible that I'm making a major mistake by staying, by not telling you the whole truth about what happened down the street. But I'm pretty sure you don't tell me every detail of your kills, either.

My phone chimes, and it startles me. I realize it isn't the cops at all I should be worried about. I roll over, pick up my phone and I read the text. IT'S SOPHIA: MEET ME AT YOUR BACK DOOR.

~

I PUT ON COFFEE, AND SOPHIA SITS AT OUR DINING ROOM table. Her eyes are wild, her hair matted. Her clothes are muddy, and she's aged thirty years in the short hours since I saw her last.

"Tell me everything," I say, and then I look up at the ceiling. "Quietly."

"I—I," she starts, and she cups the mug in her palms. She's shaking, and I ought to offer her a blanket, but I need answers before I can really care.

"Start from the beginning," I tell her. "It's all right," I lie. "You're safe."

"I killed them."

"Why would you do that?"

"I can't believe I killed them."

"What happened, Sophia?" I demand. "After I left."

'They would've told," she says.

"Would've told what?"

"About you. And about Monique."

"About Monique? What about Monique?"

"Don't worry, Mrs. Kate. I won't tell. Monique did bad things. She was different."

"What do you mean, *bad things*?"

She takes a sip from her cup. "It doesn't matter anymore," she says taking a sip. "I know you killed her," she tells me, and she's wrong but she's close. Too close for my comfort.

I bit my lip and I test her. "I didn't kill her."

She looks away. "It's okay," she says, eventually meeting my eye. She wears a dazed expression. "I'm just happy we can be together now."

"Why did you kill those girls?"

She smiles, and it lights up her whole face. "So they wouldn't tell the police about you. Small sacrifices, you know. I read that in one of your books."

"My books?"

"On parenting," she shifts her position. "I need this job… and I could be a part of your family. I never had a mother. But I like the way you do it. You and Mr. Jude. You protect your kids. You make sacrifices. It's important."

I fold my lips and I nod, as though what she's just told me makes perfect sense. And the messed-up part is, it kind of does. But I know crazy when I see it, and it has just shown up here in our kitchen. It's sitting in our chair, drinking our tea, asking to be let in. Only it's already in, and now we have a situation on our hands. My mind races and then it slows. I think of the children sleeping upstairs, and sacrifice knows no limits. Apparently, not for her, and certainly not for me. And all I can think about is how in the world I'm going to tell you. Also, I realize you're right about one thing: we don't need a nanny. Certainly not now, and maybe not ever again.

⁓

I CLEAR THE MUGS OFF THE TABLE AND TIDY UP THE KITCHEN. I can feel Sophia's eyes on me.

"Why don't you let me get that, Mrs. Kate?" she smiles. "That's what I'm here for."

"It's fine," I say, waving her off. I look over at the microwave. The clock reads 3:52 a.m., which leaves me only a few hours before the kids are up, to figure something out. I place the cups in the dishwasher and close the door, and then I turn toward Sophia. "Why don't you shower?" I say. "I'll bring in some fresh clothes."

"I had to hide in the woods."

"I can see that," I say, not sure why she's telling me something that is apparent.

"I'm good at hiding."

"It's a good thing."

She smirks. "I learned from you."

"Of course, you did," I tell her, because what else is there to say?

She stands and dusts herself off, shuffling mud off of her and onto the floor. I watch as she looks down at the mess she's made and then she looks at me.

She takes a deep breath in. "I'm so sorry," she cries, and she falls to the floor. "I'm so sorry. I'll clean it up, I promise. Just please don't make me leave. Please."

"Sophia. Shh," I whisper, but it's useless because her sobs only grow louder.

"I didn't mean to do it, I swear. I didn't mean to," she cries, repeating the same sentence over and over until I'm left with no choice but to sink to the floor and take her face in my hands.

She weeps and she weeps until eventually my legs go numb, and I have to shake her off of me. I never did care much for the criers.

"I'm so sorry, Mrs. Kate. I promise I'll be good," she tells me snot running down her chin.

"It's fine, Sophia," I say. "Just take a shower," I order, my tone commanding, in charge. She perks up, and it's as though she realizes this was the missing piece all along.

"Use the downstairs bathroom," I say, wiping my forehead. "I'll go up and get you some fresh clothes."

~

I OPEN BATHROOM DOOR SLOWLY, AND I PLACE THE CLOTHING

on the edge of the counter. I can see Sophia's silhouette from inside the shower, and for a moment I hesitate.

"I'm sorry for crying," she says, catching me off guard. Her nose is stuffy, her tone soft.

I can hear the water run over her and splatter against the tile, and there it is, that urge. It never goes away; it's forever creeping up. She sighs, bringing me back to the present, to the task at hand. "I know you're not good with emotions. But I promise we can work it out."

I raise my brow instinctively, even though I know she can't see from inside the shower. "I was thinking about running out for breakfast. Are you interested in coming along?"

"Sure," she says, and I hear a hint of amusement in her tone. I turn to go, and that's when I see it.

Written on the mirror are the words: *I've got my eye on you.*

"What is this on the mirror?" I ask, one hand on the doorknob, one hand balled in a fist.

She laughs. "A joke."

"It's not funny."

"No?"

"So you knew about the letters, then?"

"Ann and Stanley thought it was a joke. They liked to talk about it…"

"I see," I tell her, and I feel my hand slip from the knob, desire pulling me back in.

～

BLOOD RUNS DOWN THE DRAIN, TINGEING THE CLEAR WATER, turning it pink. "Why Sophia?" I ask. "Why did it have to be this way? I almost liked you," I tell her, and she stares up at me, her expression pained, as it should be, the light in her eyes fading.

She digs her nails into my hand and I pull the towel tighter on her throat. She doesn't scream, and I didn't want it to be this way. I want to hear her talk. I want answers. I want to know why she didn't tell me about the Morrises, why she kept it from me, why she killed those girls. I want to know why this whole thing happened. I want to pick her brain for a bit, to understand Anne and Stanley and why they did what they did, I want to ask if crazy begets crazy. I want to get her take on whether like attracts like, and if this is how we ended up here, soaking wet, tangled together on the shower floor. But maybe not every question gets an answer. Maybe sometimes it is what it is. And you do what you do, and you let it be.

Also, there's the fact that you and the kids are upstairs, and it takes at least three minutes to strangle a person. Thinking about what I'll need to do afterward to get rid of her, I realize answers will require patience, and no one's got time for that. In turn, I pull tighter on the towel, giving it everything I've got. I watch her eyes roll back into her head. When her face goes slack, I give it another minute, my biceps burning. I embrace the pain and I count. When I get to sixty, I check her pulse. I count again just to be sure.

Afterward, I stand over her, towel-drying her naked, lifeless body. Then I change into the clothes I brought down, pleased with myself because you say I don't plan ahead. Then I drag her through the kitchen and out into the garage, where I place her in your trunk. It's not that I made the conscious decision to put you out, it's just that your car is lower to the ground and killing a person is hard work.

~

CHAPTER TWENTY-TWO

JUDE

You sit with your legs crossed on the therapist's couch and I can tell you're wondering why I brought you here. "I'm pleased to finally meet you," the therapist says, and I watch as you shake her hand. I can tell that you're sizing her up, and I can also see that you don't like her. It's nice when we're in agreement on things.

She looks down at her tablet. "It is wonderful to see you again, Mr. Riley," she says as she touches her neck.

She meets my eye and she smiles. "I wasn't sure you'd be back," she adds, as though there's some sort of secret between the two of us.

I look at you, and you're aware that she is flirting, but rather than look angry, I'd peg you as amused.

She clears her throat and meets your eye. "As you know, Jude has applied for a position within our firm, and it's customary that we meet and evaluate the wives of all of our candidates. I appreciate you being here."

"Your husband is really quite something."

"Is he?"

"He is. He's perfect for the job."

"Huh," you say, and you're doing your best not to show your cards, but you aren't that good, not when it comes to what's yours.

"You don't think so?"

You smile and you look over at me. "Actually, before you brought it up, I wasn't aware he was looking for a 'job,'" you tell her, and I like the way you emphasize your words.

"Oh," she says and she zeros in on me. "In that case, what did you think you were here for then?"

You shrug. "Marital counseling."

Mrs. Edwards-Steinbeck shifts to face me. She tilts her head and narrows her gaze. "You're a clever one, Mr. Riley," she says, and I'm not sure what she means but I won't argue her point.

"Why do you think you need this job?" you ask me, not taking your eyes off of her.

"So I can be home more."

I watch as you purse your lips. "I guess that makes sense…"

"Why would the two of you need marital counseling?" the therapist addresses you.

You smile. "I can think of a few reasons."

Mrs. Edwards-Steinbeck raises her brow, "And? Would you mind naming them? You mentioned marital counseling…I've been married for a few decades… maybe I can help."

"Somehow I doubt that."

She shifts crossing and uncrossing her legs. "Try me."

I watch you as you glance at her ring finger and then up at her eyes. You're ready to go to war. "Have you ever worried that your husband might kill you, Mrs—" you pause, and you look down at her nameplate, and then back at her. "Steinbeck?"

The therapist pats her hair and looks over at me. She shakes her head. "No, I can't say I have."

"Why would Jude want to kill you?" she asks, and her voice lingers on my name.

"Ask *him*."

She looks over at me and she actually smirks. It was probably a bad move on her part. "Why would you kill your wife?"

I shrug.

She looks back at you. You bite your lip. "I guess a better question to ask is, why wouldn't he?"

She looks surprised. "And by that you mean what, exactly?"

"He's a killer. It's what he does," you answer, and then you stand, straightening your skirt. "And for what it's worth, I think you should give him the job," you say, and then you look from her, to me, and back at her. "He's very good at deception."

"Before you go, Kate," she calls. "May I just make an observation?"

You don't answer, but you wait.

She takes that for what it is, permission. "You don't seem very supportive of your husband's decision to take this job."

You smile. *Bingo.* "That's why they pay you the big bucks."

She sets her tablet down, and she doesn't look at you when she speaks. "And why is that? Why aren't you supportive?"

You start to go, but you stop, apparently to study a painting on the wall.

"You know what I think?" you say to her, but your eyes never leave the painting. "I think you ask the wrong questions."

"Oh?" she says, and she's looking at me. "What should I be asking?"

You turn to her. "Why my husband would want this job in the first place."

She shifts again, and touches her hair. I think you make her nervous. "I'm afraid I'm not following, Mrs. Riley…"

You walk over to the door. You turn and look back at me. I watch your hand as it grips the handle, and you're fuming. I expected nothing less. "My husband is a very good liar. Really," you add, "that's about all you need to know."

~

YOU WAIT IN THE CAR FOR ME, AND WHEN I CLIMB IN THE driver's seat it's clear by the way your arms are crossed that you're mad as hell.

"Are you hungry?" I ask.

You don't answer. "Good," I say. "Because the therapist is on her way out. "We're taking her to lunch to celebrate my offer."

You make eye contact for a brief second, and then you offer a fake, fuck you smile.

You want to fight, but you don't. I turn and move my laptop out of the back seat, and place it at your feet. My hand touches your leg, and you look up at me.

Your face is soft when it should be hard. "I just want what's best for us, Kate."

"This is not it," you say, your eyes on the doors to the building. You don't look at me when you speak. "You can't take this job."

"And why is that?" I ask, both surprised and not.

You purse your lips, and then you shift in my direction but only a little. "It's not who you are. You're not the kind of man who answers to other people. You like being on your own…"

"I like being with you—or at least I recall it being that way, once upon a time."

"Is that so?"

"Yes."

"All we do is argue. Nothing I do makes you happy—it's like you want me to be someone, something I'm not."

"No one is perfect," I tell you.

"I'm tired of fighting. I miss being happy. I miss us. The way we used to be—before things got crazy with the kids and the neighbors. Before we tried so hard to fit in."

"Before *you* tried so hard to fit in."

You look up at me then, your expression serious. "It's not just me. It's you, too. That's why we're here. That's why you want this job. You think it'll make things better. You think that if you're around more—if you change who you are and what makes you, well, you— then I'll be happy. But that's where you're wrong. I don't want to be happy. I want to be free. I want the same for you."

I swallow. "We can fix this, Kate."

"How?"

I offer a slight smile, trying to lighten the mood. "I can think of a few ways."

"Specifically?" you ask, crossing your arms. It's a valid question, but it sounds like a demand, and you're fucking with me. Also, I'd forgotten how much I like you angry.

"Are you looking for leadership?"

"Maybe I am."

"Okay. I say we settle this the easy way. Let's pretend we're strangers and meet for a drink."

You roll your eyes but you play along. "When?"

"Tomorrow evening. At The Driscoll."

Your eyes fall to the floorboard. "Fine."

I grin, hoping you'll notice, "It's settled then."

"I don't know..." you sigh, not ready to raise the white flag. "You don't trust me, Jude. And that's a problem."

"You're right," I offer, and it's sincere. I study your profile, and I hate seeing you sad. Angry, I can take. It turns me on. But I never want to make you sad. "Look—" I interject. "I know things have been a bit fucked up lately but—"

The shrink surprises me when she opens the door, interrupting me, interrupting us. "Where should we go?" I ask when she's settled in the back seat.

I watch in the rearview mirror as she checks the time on her phone. "How about that diner my husband is always talking about?"

"That place? It's a ways out there... Are you sure we have time?" I ask, because you can lead a horse to water, and apparently you can make him drink.

"We've got time," she says, and I realize that her piece of shit, business- stealing husband was right about one thing: jealousy does a person good. Because for the first time all day you actually smile.

❦

"WHY, KATE? WHY?" I DEMAND. YOU DON'T OFFER AN answer, you simply stare straight ahead and smile. Elizabeth Edwards-Steinbeck is pounding on the trunk, her belly full of the best French toast she said she'd ever had. She's terrified, and angry, and apparently immune to roofies. I can't help but blame you for that. It was your idea to drug her. Not to harm her, you said, just to have a little fun. Just to put her in her place. Turns out, you don't like it when people talk down to you and flirt with your man. That I don't blame you for.

But you couldn't know my plan, just as I couldn't know that we should have gone with something stronger. We have a live one on our hands. I can tell because she's not passed out— she's pleading, threatening, squirming— switching her tactics roughly every three and a half seconds, not only because she's locked in a confined space but because she's in there with a dead body, and I swear this feels like deja vu.

"What are we going to do with her?" you ask, deferring the question.

I shrug. "I just wish you'd informed me there was another dead girl in my trunk."

"I just wish you hadn't tried to trick me into marriage counseling, knowing full well I'd have to kill your shrink. Talk about deja vu," you say, and I hate it when you read my mind.

I look over at you. "You know how I feel about killing women."

"Maybe that's why you keep me around..."

"No," I tell you. "But it's a perk."

You shift in your seat. "Why am I killing her—aside from the fact that she gets off on flirting with other people's husbands?"

I focus on the road. "Because you like killing people."

"No," you tell me. "That's not it. You don't do anything without a reason."

I can't help but look at you. "You're right. I need her to get to him. It's a job."

"*Him* being her husband"

"Obviously."

"So you never intended to work for them? You weren't in it for the job?"

"No."

I see you frown in my periphery. "Then why lie?" You purse your lips. "I mean...this seems a little extreme, even for you."

I smile, and I love it when you're hardcore. "Why don't you tell me how you really feel?"

"I just want the truth. I want to understand…"

I sigh. Of course you do. "They're making bad deals… stealing business… the list goes on. But the gist is…it's some pretty dirty shit."

You turn your head in order to listen. The pounding has stopped and the moaning, the pleading takes over. You don't like it when people beg. Give it three minutes and it'll change, I want to tell you but I don't.

"I guess I just don't get it, that's all—why go about all this the hard way? It feels…dramatic. You know, a little bit like unnecessary kidnapping…that's not your style. You don't do anything without reason."

"It's just a means to an end, that's all."

"That makes sense," you say, and you exaggerate, you little smart-ass you.

"It's just been one thing after another over the past few weeks. I can't always handle everything at once. This was a big job. So I had to put it on the back burner. Sometimes you have to make sacrifices."

"Hmmm," you murmur, and you want more. You want me to spell it out, and so I do.

"Also, I had to make sure before I invited you in to help."

"Make sure of what?

"That you and I were going to work it out."

"What does that matter?"

I look over at you. "It's all that matters."

~

EPILOGUE

JUDE

It takes the whole of five months after that shit storm to get back on track, to get happy again. Or more likely, as happy as the two of us can get. But we manage. Ironically, it's summer that nearly did us in, but it's fall and winter that bring us back to ourselves, back to each other. It would be nice to say that all of our problems are solved, that everything is fixed. But life isn't like that. We are never going to be the kind of people who agree on much, you and I. If I know us, I know it will be a fight until the end. But the good news is, there isn't another person on this planet I'd rather duke it out with. You and me, we share the same agenda. Different motives, often— but the same goal, nonetheless. We want to make the world a better place, and like most people, we want it our way. The trouble is, not everyone gets to have it their way.

That's where you and I come in. We're the choosers, the fixers, the doers—motivated by something bigger than ourselves, and sometimes that something gets in the way. My father always said: if you're going to enter the ring make sure you go in with an opponent who forces you to level up. Better to lose than to get a lazy win.

And I've never found that to be as true as I have over the past year, both in love and in life. Marriage, and mating—make no mistake, it's a game. A game in which you need a good match, because otherwise what's the point? You and me, we like to outdo each other. Sometimes we win. Sometimes we lose. But losing doesn't mean you quit. It just means it's time for a new game.

My father told me that a long time ago. It was too bad he couldn't take his own advice. Maybe that's a part of it. Maybe wisdom only comes from defeat. And defeated he was. He lost and he knows it. He made his choice— he fucked up—he let a woman bring him down, and it cost him everything. I don't fault him for that. After all, who am I to point fingers about what's wrong and right? I understand why he made the choice he did. Driven by passion— he didn't see another way out. A lot of killers feel that way. Running out of options, sitting at rock bottom, it's a bad place to be. It's why people do terrible things.

Thankfully for you, I am not my father.

∼

THE CLOCK STRIKES MIDNIGHT, WE TOAST WITH CHAMPAGNE, and I lean in for a kiss. You take my face in your hands, and kiss me back hard. For a moment you pull away but then you lean in again, taking my bottom lip between your teeth. You're a little bit tipsy, but hell, everyone is.

"Get a room," someone calls. The Morgans are hosting the annual neighborhood New Year's Eve party this year, seeing that the Morrises are six feet under. It sounds like Todd Morgan speaking, although I'm too busy looking at you to care.

Your eyes sparkle, and maybe it's the champagne and maybe it's not. "You look more beautiful than ever," I tell you, and you laugh.

"To another year," you say, clinking your glass with mine.

"To another year," I say, and I study your face.

"What was your number?" you ask.

I lean in closer and whisper in your ear. "Ninety-one."

You jut out your bottom lip and you pull back. "Impressive."

"Yours?"

Your face lights up. "One hundred and two."

"Not bad," I say, and it isn't.

"Looks like I won," you say, taking a sip off your champagne flute.

"Looks that way," I say, and I lie. In truth, my number was 114, but I let you believe because life works better that way. I don't tell you that I've checked your notes just to ensure that I come up with a lesser number. Some things don't need to be said, and love is about going the extra mile. I take your hand in mine. "But isn't that what it's all about, anyway?"

"Winning?"

I shake my head, and I study your face. "Sacrifice."

"Something like that," you say, and then you smile, and it lights up my whole world.

"Do you wanna dance?" I ask, nodding toward the dance floor.

"It's all I want to do."

Later, stepping off of the dance floor, the host Todd Morgan grabs my forearm.

"What's your secret?" he smiles, and then he looks from me to you. I tilt my head just slightly, and he drops his hand from my arm. "I'm asking for a friend."

You lean over me, look him dead in the eye, and you handle this one like a champ. "We'll never tell."

A NOTE FROM BRITNEY

Dear Reader,

I hope you enjoyed reading *Dead In The Water*. If you have a moment and you'd like to let me know what you thought, feel free to drop me an email (britney@britneyking.com).

Writing a book is an interesting adventure, but letting other people read it is like inviting them into your brain to rummage around. *This is what I like. This is the way I think.*

That feeling can be intense and interesting.

Thank you, again for reading my work. I don't have the backing or the advertising dollars of big publishing, but hopefully I have something better... readers who like the same kind of stories I do. If you are one of them please share with your friends and consider helping out by doing one (or all) of these quick things:

1. Drop me an email and let me know what you thought.

britney@britneyking.com

2. Visit my Review Page and write a 30 second review (even short ones make a big difference).

http://britneyking.com/aint-too-proud-to-beg-for-reviews/

Many readers don't realize what a difference reviews make but they make ALL the difference.

3. If you'd like to make sure you don't miss anything, to receive an email whenever I release a new title, sign up for my new release newsletter at:

https://britneyking.com/new-release-alerts/

Thanks for helping, and for reading *Dead In The Water.* It means a lot. Be sure to check out the second book in my latest series, *Come Hell or High Water* at the end of this book, as well as via your favorite retailer.

Britney King

Austin, Texas

December 2017

ABOUT THE AUTHOR

Britney King lives in Austin, Texas with her husband, children, two dogs, one ridiculous cat, and a partridge in a peach tree.

When she's not wrangling the things mentioned above, she writes psychological, domestic and romantic thrillers set in suburbia.

Without a doubt, she thinks connecting with readers is the best part of this gig. You can find Britney online here:

Email: britney@britneyking.com
Web: https://britneyking.com
Facebook: https://www.facebook.com/BritneyKingAuthor
Instagram: https://www.instagram.com/britneyking_/
Twitter: https://twitter.com/BritneyKing_
Goodreads: https://bit.ly/BritneyKingGoodreads
Pinterest: https://www.pinterest.com/britneyking_/

Happy reading.

ACKNOWLEDGMENTS

First, thank you for reading my work.

To my friends in the book world—you guys are the icing on the cake. From fellow authors to the amazing bloggers who put so much effort forth simply for the love of sharing books, thank you.

A special thanks to my very first readers, Samantha Wiley, Brandi Reeves, Jennifer Hanson, and Hunter King. Thank you for making me better. Also, to my advance reader team, I'm grateful.

Again—because it deserves to be said twice, I'd like to thank the readers. For every kind word, for simply reading... you guys are the best.

ALSO BY BRITNEY KING

The Social Affair

The Social Affair is an intense standalone about a timeless couple who find themselves with a secret admirer they hadn't bargained for. For fans of the anti-heroine and stories told in unorthodox ways, the novel explores what can happen when privacy is traded for convenience. It is reminiscent of films such as One Hour Photo and Play Misty For Me. Classics. :)

Water Under The Bridge | Book One
Dead In The Water | Book Two
Come Hell or High Water | Book Three
The Water Series Box Set

The Water Trilogy follows the shady love story of unconventional married couple—he's an assassin—she kills for fun. It has been compared to a crazier book version of Mr. and Mrs. Smith. Also, Dexter.

Bedrock | Book One
Breaking Bedrock | Book Two
Beyond Bedrock | Book Three
The Bedrock Series Box Set

The Bedrock Series features an unlikely heroine who should have known better. Turns out, she didn't. Thus she finds herself tangled in a messy, dangerous, forbidden love story and face-to-face with a madman hell-bent on revenge. The series has been compared to Fatal Attraction, Single White Female, and Basic Instinct.

Around The Bend

Around The Bend, is a heart-pounding standalone which traces the journey of a well-to-do suburban housewife, and her life as it unravels, thanks to the secrets she keeps. If she were the only one with things she wanted to keep hidden, then maybe it wouldn't have turned out so bad. But she wasn't.

Somewhere With You / Book One
Anywhere With You / Book Two
The With You Series Box Set

The With You Series at its core is a deep love story about unlikely friends who travel the world; trying to find themselves, together and apart. Packed with drama and adventure along with a heavy dose of suspense, it has been compared to The Secret Life of Walter Mitty and Love, Rosie.

∼

In the tradition of *Gone Girl* and *Behind Closed Doors* comes a gripping, twisting, furiously clever read that demands your attention, and keeps you guessing until the very end. For fans of the anti-heroine and stories told in unorthodox ways, *Come Hell or High Water* delivers us the perfect dark and provocative villain.

"I've been studying her for weeks. I know how she takes her coffee, the color she prefers on her nails, the way her mouth moves when she sleeps. I don't know what she looks like when she's happy. But I will."

When Cheryl Steinbeck-Edwards makes the decision to get in a car with a potential contractor, meticulous hitman Jude Riley and his lovely wife Kate, it appears to be the perfect partnership. Turns out, nothing is perfect, and getting in that car was a poor choice, to say the least.

When Kate decides not to kill the woman, as she and her husband agreed, a series of events, some might even call it karma, conspire to turn their worst fears turn into reality.

COME HELL OR
HIGH WATER

BRITNEY KING

COPYRIGHT

For the readers—
It all started with a book.

PREFACE

There's a woman not long dead
who rests down
by the water's edge.
Her final words were,
"Please. Just get it over —"
She never did get the second half
of her sentiment out.
I made sure she never would.
Some things are best left unsaid.
In the end, it didn't matter anyhow.
I knew she was ready to die.
And she knew it, too.

⁓

There's a woman who rests down
by the water's edge.
She wasn't good for us,
but you tried to make it okay.
It cost us—that's on you.
I knew keeping her was wrong.
I just wish you had, too.

⁓

CHAPTER ONE

KATE

AFTER

Life often has a funny way about leading you around to where it wants you to be, at least that's what I've come to find. Speaking of finding things, I know I shouldn't be here. It was a risky move, coming, but at the same time—a promise is a promise. I said I'd take care of this, and I'm determined to hold up my end of the deal. Still, that doesn't mean I have to like it.

Get in. Get out. I repeat this to myself over and over, step by step, until I reach the front porch. When my foot hits the first stair, I pause and glance backward over my shoulder. I just need a moment. The sun is bright today, but the sun is deceptive. It isn't warm; there's a chill in the air, and it's the kind that stings when it hits my skin. The wind whips my hair, covering my face; it has little concern for anything that stands in its way. I brush it back and climb the remaining steps. If only it weren't so cold out. I might've stayed put; I might've changed my mind. I might've gone back home to you.

Ring the bell, I say to myself. *Lift your finger and push the bell.* I know what to do; I just can't make myself do it. Thankfully, the decision is made for me. Before I gather the nerve to press the bell, the door swings open, and something shifts —and it isn't the wind. It's something within me, and that something feels a whole lot like my resolve. I swallow hard, trying to dislodge the lump that's formed in my throat. It doesn't help. Turns out, a little saliva has nothing on fear, and so the lump remains. Also, I'm standing face to face with him, and it feels like a long time coming.

Up close, he's different than I imagined. That's not to say that I really imagined much. I guess I'd just expected a little more from her, is all. Someone not so… ordinary looking, would be one way to put it. If this is her type, then what do I know? Maybe it's the gray that peppers the dark hair at his temples, or maybe it's the way his smile turns downward, but he seems older than I thought he'd be.

He doesn't speak immediately. He greets me with a nod, and we stare at each other in some sort of silent standoff, sizing one another up, or at least I assume that's what we're doing. I wonder if he can read the sleepless nights on my face, or see the effects of the twelve pounds that I've lost in just two weeks alone. Can he see the guilt in my ashen face? Can he feel the sadness in the pit of my stomach? Does he see the despair in my eyes? Does he know that I'm a failure, as a mother, a wife, a friend? If he can, he doesn't say. He simply moves to the side, allowing me to slip by and into his world as though we've known each other our whole lives.

For a moment, I consider that he isn't the man I've come to see. But as I pass, I notice in his expression a mild curiosity, the kind she described, and I realize it's definitely him. Also, that I shouldn't have come.

What are you doing, Kate? It's your voice, not mine, that I hear and it suddenly becomes clear—really clear—that no one knows I'm here. Still, I can't help myself. I showed up for a reason, and I know I won't be able to forgive myself if I don't see this through, and so when he rounds the corner, and he beckons me to follow, I do. Better to get it over with and get on with your day, his posture seems to say.

The inside of the place is darker and stuffier than it looked from the outside. I was pleased to see when I Googled the address, that he offices out of an old home. I've always had a thing for old houses, and this one does not disappoint. From the curb, it is apparent it is well kept, but in here, it feels empty—lonely—in need of something I can't quite name. *Just like her.*

Making my way through the hall, I wonder if he lives here, in this old house, with the loneliness and the unnameable things. I almost ask, but he ushers me into our final destination, a second living area which has been converted into an office, and I think better of it. The room is smartly decorated, which makes sense, considering his connection to her. But maybe I'm projecting. If so, I've certainly come to the right place. I laugh softly at the thought, maybe because I'm nervous, or maybe it's the book that catches my eye.

In any case, there's not much to the space, aside from a desk, a small couch, and an armchair. He clears his throat and then shuffles his feet, and it suddenly occurs to me that I haven't got all day, and I probably ought to get on with it.

He doesn't say so, but his straight back and upturned mouth give the impression that he holds all the answers one could ever need, tucked neatly into his back pocket, and it momentarily crosses my mind that maybe I don't really want to know them after all.

I can feel his eyes on me, which is why I meet his gaze. His expression appears to say that he expects I'll be comfortable here, and I hope he is right. Does he know I can't decide whether I've come to kill him or simply to satisfy my curiosity? It's hard to say. What I do know is the intensity with which he studies me also makes me want to go, to press rewind and reverse every mistake I've likely just made by coming here. But I won't. I can't.

When I step further into the office, he follows. I glance toward his desk. I don't see any therapist-type things on it— there aren't files— and there aren't pens or notepads. Instead, it's covered in books, stacked neatly in rows. I inhale, and if life changing had a scent, it would smell like this. It's *The Great Gatsby* that caught my eye. The irony of the past, beckoning. "It was my father's," he says, clearing his throat, and I don't know if he's referring to the book or the desk, and I don't ask.

I shift, but I make a mental note to get a better look at the selection of books he owns before our time is up. It's interesting; I don't know what I'll find on that desk, only that it'll be something brilliant, probably something a little uncomfortable, like *Lolita* or *The Scarlett Letter*, the type of book that stretches the reader. He sees me looking, and he smiles. I know that whatever is in those stacks, I won't find anything simple or cozy or sweet, but rather something in your face— direct— the kind of book that asks something of you. *Set your feelings aside,* it says. *Let me take the lead; I'll show you how this goes.*

He closes the door behind him, and I wonder whether this is customary—a convention to make me more comfortable— to get me to open up, because it doesn't appear there are any other occupants in the house. Also, up close, he's tall. Taller than I realized. Taller than you, even. He moves quickly across the room, like a cat, and takes a seat. He doesn't motion for me to sit; he just assumes I'll know what to do. He's all business, until he isn't.

"Would you care for something to drink?" he asks, raising his brow. "Tea? Coffee? Vodka?"

His voice is low; it resonates somewhere deep inside, bounces around and lodges itself just where it wants to be. Like yours. I glance at an imaginary watch on my wrist. "It's a little early for vodka," I say.

"Just barely," he tells me, and the words catch on his lips and hang there. I don't respond. I study his hands instead. They seem like capable hands—like yours, like hers, I think. He folds them in his lap; he isn't one for small talk. When I look up, I shift my focus to his face. I'm trying to get a sense of the direction he'll take, but all I see is nothing, and I can't guess which way things will go. *He knows her, too.* "So—Mrs. —"

"Water," I interject, and my voice comes out smooth, just the way I wanted it.

"Water. That's right. I remember now from your email," he says and then he pauses to look up at me, peering over his glasses as he does. "What an interesting name…" he adds and then he furrows his brow as though he's just remembered something long forgotten. I've seen that look before. You have it down to an art.

Still, he doesn't take his eyes off mine. "But I bet you've heard that before."

"A time or two, yes," I answer, averting my gaze. I don't mean to look away, but those eyes of his, they burn. They're the kind that see through you, and I don't particularly want to be seen through. He nods curtly, and he waits before he speaks again, although I'm not sure for what.

"Anyway," I say. "It's Ginny," I mention, because silence seems like the wrong way to go. I offer the name because I need something to fill the space, but also because it feels good rolling off my tongue. *Ginny.* It's a girlish name, one that reminds me of someone who's perpetually young— bright— sunny and happy. A person named Ginny could never do anything bad. I picture her in my mind. She would be nothing at all like me.

"Okay then, Ginny—" he starts. I know I am supposed to maintain eye contact, and so I do. It isn't easy. "You've come a long way," he says, and he's only partially right.

"Yes," I tell him.

"And you mentioned in your email that you have something of mine?"

"Yes," I say, bending down to remove the book from my bag. I look up at him, and suddenly it seems odd that he didn't ask for it at the door. But then, I knew he wouldn't. He may not be the kind for small talk, but he's not impolite either. He watches me carefully. I lean forward and hand it to him.

He takes it from me carefully, as though it might slip through his fingers. I watch as he studies the cover and flips it over in his hands. "*Lady Chatterley's Lover,*" he whispers, running his fingers along its edge. He glances up suddenly. "Where did you get this?"

"I found it on a bench in the park..."

"Which park?"

"Downtown."

He cocks his head. "Where downtown?"

"Lou Neff..."

"Huh," he says.

"I was running the trail—I stopped to stretch and there it was..."

He flips open to the title page. "And you saw my name here," he says pointing.

I grit my teeth. "I Googled you. I hope you don't mind."

"Not at all," he tells me and exhales. I hear relief in it. "This book is very special to me."

"I figured as much..." I say. "Seeing that your name is inside."

He looks away again, and it doesn't escape me that maybe he knows I'm lying.

"It says, *I love you always*. I figured it might've been a gift."

"Yes," he replies. "It was." I can see that he doesn't want to say more—that he isn't going to— but at the same time, I'm not ready for the conversation to end.

"I'm glad it's found its way back," I say.

He nods, I smile. "Anyway—seeing that you're a therapist and all, I was wondering if you might have time for a quick question?"

He nods once again, as though maybe he were expecting as much. He doesn't tell me I've come to the right place. He doesn't reassure me, not like most people would. He isn't trying to sell me, and I respect this about him.

"I've been wondering how one knows..." I start, and then I stop and twist my hair around one finger. I pull it tight and then let go. "I was wondering how one might know—or— rather, I guess what I'm trying to say is—" I pause to take a deep breath. "I was wondering how someone really knows when it's time to end a relationship."

He tilts his head, like this is the most interesting thing he's heard in a long time, when we both know it isn't. "That's an interesting question."

I offer a nervous smile. "An interesting question that has an answer?"

"Well," he begins, and he pauses to rub his jaw. "How long have you been asking yourself whether or not you should end things?"

"Eight months, two weeks, five days."

He raises his brow, drops his hand. "That's pretty exact."

"Yes."

"Are you always so precise?"

"Lately..."

"I see," he says. Then he narrows his eyes, his gaze boring holes through me. "And what would you say has changed?"

"Everything."

"I see," he tells me thoughtfully, but he's wrong. He doesn't see.

When I don't say anything he adjusts his glasses. "Do you want to extrapolate?" he asks, and there isn't any emotion on his face as he says it, and I want to know more about how he hides his emotions so well. All of a sudden, he reminds me of you, and I'm not sure what to make of this either. I'm not sure what I expected to find, coming here, only that somehow this revelation isn't helping any.

I shrug slightly and then tuck my hands between my thighs. "I just thought maybe there was a way to know..."

"Do you still love this person?"

"More than is good for me," I reply, and the words slice through my insides on their way out.

"And yet you feel unsure as to whether you want to stay in the relationship," he states. Then he pauses, again. He likes to leave space between his comments, crevices one can just fall into. It's a minefield, navigating all that space. It's a question, but not a question. It's brilliant, is what it is.

I nod my head. "Yes."

"May I ask why?"

"I guess you could say it's no longer compatible with my lifestyle." And there it is, each syllable taking all of me with them when they go. I don't know what I feel as they hang in the air between us. Maybe nothing. Maybe something. Maybe I just needed to say the words. Still, I wish I could take them back, suck them in, make it not so. But I can't. Turns out, most things, you can't take back—what's done is done.

"I'm sorry," he tells me, and it's genuine.

"Me too," I say, and I look away.

"Letting go of someone special can be very difficult."

I swallow hard, and the tears come even though I don't want them to. It's like everything that's happened—it all hits me at once, and I can't help it. Not this time. I wipe my cheek with the back of my hand and then I meet his eye. "Tell me about it."

∼

Learn more at: britneyking.com

28233852R00171

Printed in Poland
by Amazon Fulfillment
Poland Sp. z o.o., Wrocław